PIPER'S
FERRY

Also by G. Clifton Wisler

The Seer
The Wolf's Tooth
The Antrian Messenger
The Raid
Buffalo Moon
Thunder on the Tennessee
Winter of the Wolf
Esmeralda
Lakota
Ross's Gap
The Return of Caulfield Blake
This New Land
Antelope Springs
The Trident Brand
A Cry of Angry Thunder
My Brother, the Wind

PIPER'S FERRY

A Tale of the Texas Revolution

G. Clifton Wisler

LODESTAR BOOKS ★ DUTTON ★ NEW YORK

Copyright © 1990 by G. Clifton Wisler

Library of Congress Cataloging-in-Publication Data

Wisler, G. Clifton.
   Piper's Ferry: a tale of the Texas Revolution / G. Clifton
Wisler.
      p.   cm.
   Summary: A fourteen-year-old ferry worker joins the army to fight
for Texas's independence.
   ISBN 0-525-67303-2
   1. Texas—History—Revolution, 1835–1836—Juvenile fiction.
[1. Texas—History—Revolution,   1835–1836—Fiction.   2. Texas—
History—To 1846—Fiction.]   I. Title.
PZ7.W78033Pi   1990   89-13555
[Fic]—dc20   CIP
                                                          AC

Published in the United States by Lodestar Books,
an affiliate of Dutton Children's Books,
a division of Penguin Books USA Inc.

Published simultaneously in Canada by
Fitzhenry & Whiteside Limited, Toronto

Editor: Rosemary Brosnan   Designer: Marilyn Granald, LMD

Printed in the U.S.A.   First Edition

10 9 8 7 6 5 4 3 2 1

for my young Texas readers,
whose support and encouragement
made Piper's Ferry *a reality*

PIPER'S
FERRY

ONE

I NEVER LAID EYES on Texas till I was nigh onto my fourteenth birthday. 'Course, Texas wasn't much of a place at all back then, and I wasn't more'n a pine shavin' myself. My tale is one of mischance and odd circumstance, as strange a story in fact as Texas's own. And I suppose it's why the two of us always felt a kind of kinship, the one for the other.

I was born up in Natchez, on the Mississippi River, in April of 1821. Hadn't been many years since ole Andy Jackson had whipped the British down at New Orleans, and I close to got myself called Victory. Now what sort of name'd that've been, Victory Piper? Luck was with me for a change, and my mama dubbed me Timothy Patrick instead.

"Scrawny thing as you were, I thought it sure you'd need a pair of patron saints to keep you from the devil's temptations!" she told me often. Then, too, she was particular fond of some Irish uncle of hers name of Tim.

As for devil's temptations, they arrived soon enough. Mama, not content with as fine a boy as I promised to be, went and hatched my brother Michael when I was two. Then, when I finally saw Michael out of baby linens, along came Agnes Elizabeth! How I survived such trials is a great mystery. Still, by the time I'd passed my sixth

Mississippi winter, I was promisin' to become a regular straw-haired terror of the river wharves.

Most days I'd escape Mama's attention and wander down to the levees to snag catfish. There were sights down there to see, too. The riverboats'd churn up the muddy bottoms, and wagons full of cotton or rice would pull up at Hurley's Landin'. Big field hands half a head taller'n a tree would haul bales up the ramps onto the steamboats. They were somethin', all muscled and hard, singin' their sad, mournful songs. I used to take 'em dippers of water when the sun was extra hot, and they'd give me a nod or a grin. Days later they'd find me down at the levee and share a tale or bring me some rotten bacon for fish bait.

Papa was a cotton buyer, and he rode here and there, makin' deals for this crop and that. More'n once he took me with him, lettin' me crawl up back of him on his big dappled gray. He was a fine horseman, Jerome Piper. And he won many a race atop that gray.

"I don't take with gamblin'," Mama scolded him after he won three silver pieces off a travelin' Spanish gentleman. "No good'll come of it, Jerome!"

"Leave me a particle of amusement, dear," he'd reply. "A gentleman has need of sport with the market doing so poorly."

In truth, racin' horses and playin' cards was just part of the trade along the river. I never knew a full-grown man didn't chew tobacco or take a hand. And Papa never bet what he couldn't lose, which was a virtue of sorts, and he won more often'n not.

I don't know what put him in mind to mount Colonel Hurley's black stallion. Satan, they called that horse, and wasn't a man south of Nashville could handle the brute. It was a bet, I suppose, and Papa wasn't one for dodgin' a challenge. He was as good a rider as I'll ever see.

Not good enough, though, it turned out.

"He had Satan a head and a half ahead of the field," Josh Pettigrew explained, "when that devil horse threw him. Wasn't a way for Ned Culver to know, and he ran right over Mr. Piper, hard and sudden-like."

Josh and the colonel brought Papa back to us in a wagon, but his ribs were stove in, and he was bleedin' from the mouth.

"Kiss the little ones for me, Mary Magdalene," he told my mama. Then he died.

I wasn't used to sadness then, bein' only six, and for weeks I went off lookin' for Papa. He wasn't atop the gray, though, nor sittin' at his desk readin' Milton.

"He's gone ahead of us to heaven," Mama told me again and again. "We'll see him when we go to glory."

I'd never heard of glory, though. All I knew was Mama cried herself to sleep, and people started comin' 'round to take the furniture. Bit by bit Papa's things disappeared. The gray vanished first. Then boots and saddles, the silver teapot, even pictures off the wall.

"I've a friend in New Orleans who will take us in," Mama finally announced in mid-summer. "It's a wide, wonderful town. From the inn you can watch ships sail down the river, Tim."

I thought it a fine notion. But I saw behind Mama's mask and read a terrible sadness. Leavin' Natchez meant leavin' Papa, too, I suppose.

"It's time we buried him," she whispered to me when Michael and I huddled together in our blankets on the deck of the steamboat that was to take us downriver.

I didn't understand. We'd buried Papa months ago.

New Orleans was a marvelous place! From the moment I stepped off the steamboat, my right hand tightly gripped by Michael and my left draggin' along a too-heavy carpetbag, I was taken by the bustle of the place. Big ships bound for distant lands stood ridin' at anchor in the basin. Side-wheelers and paddle wheelers by the score awaited passengers, discharged cargoes, or rolled along the sleepy river.

Mama found us a carriage, and the coachman took us down dusty streets lined with grand houses as big and richly decorated as Colonel Hurley's manor house back in Natchez. Only in New Orleans there were whole streets of such places, and tall stone buildin's as well. We passed by St. Louis Cathedral, built by the French way back when, and we continued on through the old quarter to a newer part of town. Buildin's there lacked the elegance of the old French section, but there was life, a sort of bustin'-out vitality even amid the pine planks and smoky tallow lamps. Mama motioned finally for the coachman to stop at a simple three-story place painted red with black trim. Over the door was a signboard with a boar's head.

"We're home," Mama announced as she carried Agnes Elizabeth out of the carriage. Michael and I followed, stunned. Home? It was a sorry-lookin' place, and an inn to boot. Mama once said she wouldn't go inside such a place if the devil himself was chasin'. Well, I learned later it was worse. There were creditors after us. Mama had hired out to cook for the place.

The wonder of New Orleans wore off fast. Michael and I together weren't much better'n a thimble of salt, and Mama's friend, the innkeeper Mr. Havers, had us slop-pin' his hogs and feedin' the chickens, scrubbin' win-dows and polishin' doorknobs, workin' ourselves thinner by the day until Mama took to worryin' after our health.

"It's a poor life I've brought you to, my dears," she sobbed often. "What will come of us all?"

Mama worked harder'n any of us, though. She cooked and washed like an ill-used slave, and afterward she read us stories and oversaw my lessons. I wasn't much for studyin' on my own, but she tied me to a chair and insisted I get along with my numbers or copy out verses I was gettin' to know by heart. Then one of our boarders, a sea captain name of Tom Fitzgerald, took an interest in me. In between salty tales of adventures on the high seas, he worked me through my math and got me through a dozen history books he borrowed off acquaintances.

"Do you have to know history to go to sea?" I asked him.

"Never hurts a man to work his mind, Tim," he told me. "Mind's like any tool, you know. Acquires rust through disuse. You have to take her out and polish her up proper. Shipshape! Then she's there to use when you've need."

"Not much need for history and figures when you slop hogs all day," I grumbled.

"You won't be doing that forever, Timmy Piper. There's another fate ahead of you. I read it in your eyes."

I didn't see it there myself, but Captain Fitzgerald spoke with a voice used to havin' his way, and there was no arguin' with him. The week before Christmas I learned what he had in mind.

"Dear ones, Captain Fitzgerald's made us an offer," Mama explained. "He's taken a fine house up on Chestnut Street, and he says it's terribly empty."

"If you're of a mind to put up with the wayward habits of an ole seadog, I'd have you fill it for me," the captain said.

Agnes Elizabeth took to bouncin' around like a ball, and Michael gave a hoot.

"You got hogs?" I asked.

"Enough to keep you busy," he answered. "But not too busy for a climb up the mast or a day at the wharves."

"I don't understand, Mama," I told her. "Why would the cap'n take us in if it's not to keep his house?"

"A man hires servants for such," Captain Fitzgerald answered, liftin' me onto one shoulder and wrappin' his spare arm around Michael. "It's a family I'm wanting."

"He's to be your new papa," Mama explained. "If you'll have him."

Well, we raised a great cry, for such a generous fate had rarely befallen us. Just three days after I celebrated my eighth birthday, Captain Tom Fitzgerald became my stepfather. In truth, though, he'd been our kin since the first time he'd rocked Agnes Elizabeth to sleep or took Mama strollin'. We left the Boar's Head for the kinder walls of 15 Chestnut Street. I never looked back.

TWO

THOSE NEXT FIVE YEARS flew by smooth as China silk. We were happy, Captain Tom and us. Our family got taller ... and bigger, too. Here was brother Michael turnin' eleven and gettin' uncomfortably close to bein' tall as me, and Agnes Elizabeth turnin' prettier every day. And that wasn't enough! Mama and the captain went and had themselves three little ones—all boys, and just as loud and stubborn as an ole Missouri-bred mule. John and Jacob and James, they were called, each just exactly two years shy of the next. Michael figured the captain arranged it that way, him likin' things orderly and such. I judged the earth just wasn't altogether able to take a new Fitzgerald every year!

Bein' older kin to four brothers and a sister was close to a full-time job, especially with Captain Tom off on his ship two months out of three. He was around often enough to apply a kindly hand when needed, to keep them or me to the proper path. Most times the captain applied that hand gingerly, a light touch to the wheel, as he called it. When a good tug or a sharp whack was needed, though, he was up to the task.

I think he put a little extra care to my direction, likely 'cause of me bein' eldest. Or maybe it was on account of my takin' to his tales and history books better'n Michael, who was fine with figures but made a muddle of every-thin' else. And the little ones, bein' so small, would get their turn later on. Mama took charge of Agnes Elizabeth, so it only left me.

"Timmy, ever given any thought to your future?" he asked me shortly after I turned thirteen.

"Well, Cap'n, I thought maybe to be one of those harbor clerks, all busy with manifests and such. Or else maybe go to a real school and learn the law. Mama always says that's a noble callin'."

"Takes a lot of money, the schooling you'd need," he explained.

"Then I suppose I'd like to go adventurin'," I told him. "Go explorin' out west like Lewis and Clark. Or go to sea like you."

I could tell he'd been waitin' for that, 'cause he jumped on it right away.

"I've got a berth aboard *Bahamas Queen* for a mess boy," he explained. "Means sayin' some good-byes, and the work'd be hard. But the boy I've had is drawing assistant engineer's wages now, and he's sure to have the makings of a mate by and by."

"What's a mess boy do?" I asked.

"Well, it's a poor job, I'll admit," he said, grinnin'. "Serves the officers their food and helps the cook. Slops out the head when it's needed, mends sails, doses the sick, and swallows all the heaped curses the youngest aboard ship can stomach. He learns the sea, though, and he knows adventure."

"No hogs to slop?"

"No, it's all salt pork," he answered, laughin'. "His is a dry berth in the day cabin, though, and if he's got eyes and ears for the mates' teaching, he'll get his navigation down and steering 'fore he's full-grown."

"Then I'm for it," I announced. "When do we take ship?"

"Week from Wednesday," he explained. "Best talk with your mama and get the little ones prepared. They're sure to miss you."

I nodded. It was a truth. I'd miss them, too, even if I'd never confess it.

So it was that I went to sea. I wasn't much of a mess boy, bein' a hair shy of five feet all stretched out toe to noggin'. And if I carried eighty pounds on my too-thin bones, it would have surprised those who saw me shirtless. I was used to rough work, though, and I hurried about my chores as I'd never done on land. I stored away the coffee and sugar as the cook, Mr. Beeks, ordered, and I rolled barrels up the gangplank straight and sure as the saltiest hand.

"Boy's a marvel, Cap'n," Mr. Roney, the first mate, proclaimed as we had our supper that final night in harbor. "He's been honed sharp by a steady hand."

"Yes, sir," the others quickly agreed.

All that was in port, though. My troubles started as we steamed down the Mississippi and out into the Gulf of Mexico. I wasn't accustomed to the ship's movements, you see. I got sick. Real sick! In point of fact, I wasn't much else.

Bein' seasick's a serious setback for a sailor. Captain Tom told me I'd get my sea legs by and by, and Mr. Beeks gave me a dose of this cure and that. Even Mr. Roney, who generally had little use for the boys aboard, helped me sling a hammock near the stack where the ship was steadiest. But in a wink I was back hung over the side, retchin' and feelin' lower'n a worm.

"Never saw the like," the captain said as we sat together in the day cabin, my pale face near green now.

★9★

"I'd never have brought you to such misery, Tim. Me, I was born upside down on a yardarm, so they say. The sea's never troubled me."

"Never troubled me, either," I said, tryin' to fight off a frown. "Not till I took leave of land."

"You'll pass the rest of the voyage in my cabin, son," he explained. "It's a fast trip to Nassau and home again. When we're back, we'll consider another course to set."

"But I've got my duties," I argued.

"They're tended, Timmy. Don't you fret yourself. The whole crew's down with worry over you, and they'd likely mutiny if I left you on duty pale and weak as you are."

"I let you down," I muttered. "And I meant to make you proud."

"Never been prouder," he said, grippin' my shoulders. "And it would've been worth a cargo of silver to have you serving me. But the sea's a trickster, you know. She won't allow a man too much good fortune."

I nodded. It wasn't so different on land. Wasn't anythin' you could do about it. You just swallowed the disappointment and went on.

I don't even remember the last half of the voyage to Nassau, nor much of the trip home. It was all a blur of bellyache and heavin' over the side. By the time we tied up at the wharf in New Orleans, my ribs hurt like somebody'd stomped on 'em, and I was down to a shadow of what little there'd been of me to start with.

"Poor Tim," Mama lamented when she heard the tale.

"You look like walkin' death," Michael told me. "A ghost, sure as day. Bet you'll be a while swappin' pirate stories, eh?"

Agnes Elizabeth offered what comfort could be found in a bowl of carrot soup, and the little ones brought me bits of dry beef and slices of bread.

"Can't blame them," Captain Tom told me when we sat together on the porch swing out back. "You look as if I've starved you."

"I'll live," I assured him. "Now the ground's not swayin', I've got my senses back."

"There's still the matter of your future, Tim. I've spoken to the lawyers over on River Street, but they want five hundred dollars to school you. The clerks aren't much better. You'd fare better upriver, in Natchez or St. Louis. Those aren't such old towns and appreciate the enterprise in a young man's eyes."

"Maybe there's other work here in New Orleans," I argued. "Joe Kelly's apprenticed himself to a cooper."

"We could have a walk through the shops if you want."

"I hate the thought of goin' off by myself," I confessed. "I guess I'm not so old as I like to tell myself."

"Plenty of time left to be a man, Tim," he replied. "Wouldn't hurt you to pass another year or so at home, studyin'. You've a good head for books, and we'd all welcome your company."

We both knew, though, that it was even harder apprenticin' a boy once he got years on him. Most tradesmen deem boys rebellious by nature and unteachable by seventeen. But when the captain and I walked the shops that next week, we met with a grim response.

"Him?" Otis Hanby gasped when we visited the sailmakers. "Why, he's spindly-legged, and his fingers are too short. I want a boy who's light on his feet and good in the lofts. This one, I hear, gets light-headed at the roll of a ship."

The cabinetmakers and ironmongers also declared me unfit.

"Look at him!" Jesse Murrow cried when we visited the printshop on Elm Street. "He's readin' the handbills!"

That's what he'd do when I needed type set. He's much too book-learned to put in a respectable day's labor. You've spoilt him for hard work, Tom."

"All he's ever known's hard work!" the captain barked. "When I first met him, nigh six years old, he was slopping the hogs and polishing brass like a lad twice his age, and bent weary like an ole washwoman! I'd take him with me 'cept the sea won't have him."

"Won't anybody have him!" Mr. Murrow said, laughin'. "Maybe hire him out as a stable hand."

I could see Captain Tom gettin' redder in the face, and it was all he could do to usher me out of that shop without breakin' somethin' over Mr. Murrow's nose.

"Pay them no mind, Timmy," the captain said as we started the long walk home. "They've spent too many years on the wharves. Boys wash up like driftwood along the river, and men grow hard hearts toward 'em."

"Maybe workin' a stable wouldn't be so bad," I told him. "I used to ride some with Papa, and I always was good with horses."

"Son, nobody signs a bond with a white boy for such work," Captain Tom explained. "Not when he can buy a slave off the Bermuda boat or off a Mississippi plantation. It's a better life you're destined to find. I won't think it otherwise."

Mama, too, refused to think of me relegated to hard labor. She had made friends at the Boar's Head, and Papa had family. As she wrote of her eldest son, Timothy Piper, and of his good character and fine work habits, I thought perhaps she had another son I'd never met. Twenty letters, I think she wrote, and only five drew answers. Three offered work, but only for a time, and the fourth spoke of hirin' me as a coach boy. The last was from Papa's Texas cousin, J. C. Piper, Esquire.

"I have only young children," Cousin J. C. explained, "and I fear I've undertaken more enterprises than my two hands can properly manage. I'm most in need of a young man with a head for business to work at the ferry I operate across the La Bahía Road crossing of the Brazos River, and to help at the public house I maintain on the west bank of that selfsame river. I couldn't offer much by way of payment, as our trade rarely pays in coin, but Texas is full of opportunity for a young man, and I would promise him a fine start in whatever of my enterprises he might choose to undertake."

"A ferry, Mama?" I asked when she read me the heart of the letter.

"It's a business like any other," Captain Tom told me. "There's need for someone to keep accounts and collect payment. And Texas is a raw, wild land."

"Wild is right!" Mama said, rubbin' her hands together. "Wild with Indians and murderers!"

"So once was most of this country," the captain pointed out. "It's a country that won't spit on learning, Mary Magdalene, and land's nearly free. I've thought of going there myself, starting a river trade."

"We could go together," I suggested.

"Not just now," my stepfather answered. "It's difficult to get a license from the Mexican government."

"It's in Mexico?" I cried.

"Yes, though there have been efforts to purchase the country. General Jackson speaks of it often."

The general was president of the whole country now, but folks in New Orleans still called him by his military title. Always would, I suppose, him havin' delivered 'em from the British and all.

"I don't speak Spanish," I said, frownin'.

"You'll be among family, in country settled by Ameri-

★13★

cans," Captain Tom assured me. "I've heard it's a garden there, as fine a country as a man might wish to see. I envy you, Tim."

"It's so far," Mama complained.

"He's not a child, dear," the captain said, takin' her hand. "It's for you to choose, though, son."

"Haven't had any other offers," I said. "I guess I'll have to go by ship, too. Still, they want me, don't you think?"

"The letter says as much," Mama agreed.

"Then there's nothin' to do but answer yes and ready myself for the trip."

"More than that, I suspect," Mama said, her eyes growin' teary. And she was right.

I set out on a crisp winter mornin', not quite fourteen and feelin' small as an ant aboard the Gulf packet boat on which Captain Tom had booked my passage. The night before, I had said my farewells, huggin' Agnes Elizabeth and the little boys and promisin' them all to write soon after my arrival. It took a bit longer to say good-bye to Michael, for the two of us had slept side by side most of our lives, shared gladness and sadness, and trusted always in the other's counsel and aid.

"You'll be the oldest now," I told him as I bundled my meager belongin's and stuffed them in a flour sack. "It's a hard job, watchin' out after everybody."

"Sure," he said, droppin' his eyes to the floor.

"You'll do all right at it, Michael. You won't be a runt like me, and you won't likely get seasick, either. Later on, when you're tall and have a hundred kids, you can come visit me, and I'll show you Texas."

"We'll never see you again," Michael lamented. "I just know it."

"That's nonsense," I argued as I steadied his tremblin'

hands. "Who's goin' to teach you to shave your first chin whiskers?"

"I hope not you," he said, managin' a grin. "You close to cut your chin off."

"See there! I'd never let you do that without bein' here to laugh about it. You come along to Texas, Michael. I won't even charge you full fare on the ferry."

"Nice of you, Timmy."

"Now it's best I get goin'. 'Cause if I wait much longer, I'll never manage it."

"Yeah, I know," he agreed, takin' my flour-sack bundle. "Cap'n Tom's waitin', too."

I met Mama on the porch. She held on to me for the longest time, just shiverin' and cryin' and not sayin' a word.

"I'll write, Mama," I promised. "And I'll watch out for trouble. I run fast, you know. They won't catch me fightin' Indians single-handed or wrestlin' gators like ole Jim Bowie."

"You're a liar, Tim Piper!" she scolded. "You'll jump on the first gator you see, and that'll be the end of you."

"Be a short meal," Michael said from the doorway.

"I feel like I'm losin' you forever," she sobbed.

"I'm not that easy to get rid of," I said. "I'll miss you."

"And I you, Timmy," she said, huggin' me so tight I thought the buttons would pop right off my shirt. Finally she released her grip, and I joined the captain atop his carriage. Michael tossed my sack in back, and I waved them all a final farewell. Then the carriage rolled into motion.

We arrived at the riverfront an hour before sailin', and Captain Tom escorted me aboard. He knew the packet's master and many of the crewmen, and he introduced me 'round. Later, I discovered a bucket in my cabin, and I smiled at the thought that he'd warned them of my accursed ill treatment by the sea.

"I don't have a lot to say," he told me as we stood together beside the gangplank that would soon slide away, cuttin' me off from what had been such a calm haven amid the storm of a troubled life. "Isn't really anything words can add to what I feel, and I read the same in your eyes. Tim, when I left home the first time my papa handed me a good skinning knife and a Bible. The Bible's packed away in your knapsack, with a few words meant for you to read at sea. I thought you might need a bigger knife, knowing you're headed to a big new country."

He passed into my hands a huge steel blade, big almost as my arm. It was a bowie special, good for carvin' anythin' that needed it, and sure to flood my head with imagined adventures. The captain knew it, for his eyes took on a sparkle.

"Thanks ... Papa," I said, grippin' his arm. He wrapped me in the other arm and held me a moment. Then he stepped back, swallowed hard, and gave me a salute.

"You've made an old seadog proud, son," he remarked. "God speed you on your way, Tim, and watch over you in peril."

With that said, he turned and clambered down the gangplank. I knew it wasn't for fear of elongatin' the partin' that he refused to look at me. It was to hide tears. Me, I kept mine inside. Instead I waved as the sailors freed the packet from the wharf. The master shouted orders. And we set off southward.

THREE

I FOUND, to my disappointment, that the small portside cabin was not mine alone. As it turned out, six of us occupied the cubicle. A pair of Texas planters shared the single berth. The rest of us—two Mississippi brothers bound to make their fortunes in Galveston, a scarecrow of a fellow named Zach Merkins, and myself, slept in blankets on the wet, rollin' deck.

Actually, I didn't sleep much. When I wasn't leanin' over the rail, my head was hangin' over the bucket.

"Lord, boy, I do believe you're greener'n a bayou frog," one of the Mississippians remarked.

"Breathe in deep and let the sea settle you, son," his brother suggested. "Let the sway of the ship get on into your bones."

I tried, but the sea had a tight grip on my innards, and it was determined to torment me further.

"Fool kid!" the taller of the planters, a gruff, gray-haired giant named Capperson, complained. "Keeps us up all the night with his heaving. Voyage's long enough if you can sleep through half of her."

"Ain't his fault," Zach declared as he helped steady me in the far corner. "I got an uncle's got the sickness. He's the same way. Uncle George cain't even ride a mule without goin' light in the head."

I think Zach and I became friends that instant. Was bound to be, I suppose, since the two of us were the only boys aboard ship save those servin' the first-class cabins or stokin' the boilers. Zach had come to New Orleans to buy tools and supplies for his papa's farm, and he was forever walkin' the deck and satisfyin' himself the hold wasn't takin' on water.

"Be a fine thing to land in Galveston with rusty plows, spoilt coffee, and ruint tobacco!" Zach explained.

"She's a steady enough ship," I assured him. "She's ridin' fair in the wind, and her engines move us along easy."

"You sound to know," he said, closin' one eye and starin' at me hard.

"I've been around ships some," I told him. "My stepfather's master of a steamer plyin' the Bahamas trade."

"And you seasick?" he cried. "Not much likely."

"No, but true just the same," I said, sighin'. "Be the ruin of me, I imagine. I had myself signed on as cabin boy, sure to have a dozen adventures 'fore I turn sixteen, only my stomach couldn't hold food on a rollin' deck. Now I'm off to Texas to work the Brazos ferry at a place called Washington Town."

"You're bound for Washington, on the Brazos?" he asked. I nodded, and he grinned. "Well, we're fated friends certain, Tim Piper. Papa's farm's just upriver a half league, and he's got me hurryin' into town for this and that all the time. Should've known it. Ain't so many Pipers in Texas, after all. You're to work for ole J. C., are you? You'll think the sea's been easy on you after a week with him."

"Oh?" I asked.

"Shouldn't speak ill of him, I suppose, not you bein' a

relation and all, but he's got a famous ill temper and a shout you can hear in Louisiana!"

"I been yelled at before," I declared.

"He'll work you down to a nub."

"I been worked before, too, Zach. I never dodged work, nor trouble, either. I figure to get along all right."

"Then you're sure to do fine on the Brazos," he said, noddin'. I watched as a flicker of mischief entered his eyes, and he grinned. "'Less the Karankawas pay you a visit."

"Who?" I asked warily.

"Indians. They get hungry and put on a raid now and again."

"It'd seem they'd worry you more'n me," I said, shakin' my head. "You've got stock on your farm."

"J. C. keeps chickens and pigs out back of the public house, but the Kranks don't much care for their taste. No, they like a different sort of meat."

"What?"

"Why, don't you know?" Zach asked. "Kranks eat people."

"Do not!" I cried, laughin' at his try at spinnin' a whopper.

"Do indeed," Zach pledged, raisin' his hand high in the air. "They're cannibals. Used to be partial to Spaniards and sailors, but now they've taken an interest in settlers, especially young ones. Ate Becky Salter a month 'fore I left for New Orleans. She was seven. They'd be hungry again by now."

"Well, they'll have a time gettin' me," I boasted, slidin' the big bowie knife out of my boot. "I can do some carvin' myself."

"Lord, I'll bet you can!" Zach howled. "That's a belly scratcher if I ever saw one!"

"Man goes to travelin', he best be able to protect himself," I said, steadyin' myself as the deck suddenly swayed.

"Good to know 'bout that knife, Tim. I got a money belt under my shirt. Could do with some armed company."

"Your papa sent you all the way to New Orleans by yourself?" I asked, surprised.

"Thieves don't expect a boy to carry money," Zach said, grinnin'. "I'm all can be spared from the work. Anyway, it's the supplies I worry after. Money won't buy much in Texas. With a plow or two, you can put a thousand acres in corn or cotton."

"Sure," I acknowledged.

That was about as long a conversation as we shared on that difficult voyage to Galveston. Sooner or later my belly would turn over, and I'd make a rush for the rail. Afterward, I'd stumble light-headed back to the cabin and try to fight off the misery. After a bit Zach would sit down beside me and spin a story about the Karankawas or some giant alligator that bit his cousin's ears off, and I'd brighten a bit.

Zach was a wonder. He was just fifteen, tall and lanky, with a man's voice and enough whiskers to shave if he had a mind to. At first look he seemed frail, but his fingers had an iron grip, and he was strong enough to throw me over one shoulder and a sack of flour over the other. It was the way he was sure of himself I admired most, though. He wasn't one you could shake. Even the Mississippians, who could rile me scarlet with their talk, had no luck with Zach Merkins. He just laughed and gave 'em that easy smile that let 'em know they best check their shoes for scorpions come daybreak.

"Trick's to keep folks guessin'," Zach told me. "Long

as they're not sure what you'll do, they're apt to give you some distance. Out in Texas, you can't expect much more'n that. Oh, you may take a beatin' or two, but people look you eye to eye."

"Even if you're runt little?" I asked.

"Copperhead's a little thing, Tim, but he's got himself a sharp bite. You got yourself a knife. Might let 'em know your bite's sharp, too."

I did as he advised, and I even pranked the Mississippians by hidin' their clothes in the longboat while they were asleep. When mornin' came, they raised a powerful ruckus and cursed Zach, me, the captain, and anybody else in sight. Mind, they didn't out and out blame anybody in particular, but when I took to whittlin' a stick and grinnin', they caught the shine in my eye. I noticed they were kinder in their comments thereafter.

We were five days sailin' to Galveston, and once we arrived, I began to wonder if it'd been worth it. In New Orleans, folks talked of the "Queen City" of Texas and such. When I stepped off the gangplank onto a rickety line of planks that passed for a wharf, I found instead a huddle of light frame buildin's strung out along several muddy wallows that the Texicans considered streets.

"Tim!" Zach called from the packet. "Don't wander!"

I waved in acknowledgment, though I had a fiery urge to go explorin'. For all its roughness, Galveston whispered in my ear of adventure. There was music in the air, and peddlers hawked all manner of wares along the landin'. I saw, too, a pair of dark-haired soldiers wearin' unfamiliar uniforms and seemingly guardin' a round-faced little man who scribbled in a pair of ledgers. It was this little man who first addressed me, and though I couldn't make out the gist of what he was sayin', I guessed the words were Spanish.

"*Pardon*," I replied, hopin' the scant French I'd picked up in New Orleans might work better'n English.

"Americano," the little man said scornfully. "Name?"

"Tim Piper," I answered.

"Full name!" he barked, "and habitation."

"I was baptized Timothy Patrick Piper," I answered. "In Natchez, Mississippi, though I've lived lately in New Orleans."

"Catholic?"

"Yes," I answered, noticin' the first particle of approval in his eye. I didn't add Captain Tom wasn't much on Mass-goin', sayin' Bible-readin' put you in better stead. Me, I didn't pass any respectable time doin' either.

"What is your purpose in coming to Texas?" the little man asked as he scribbled in his book.

"I've come to work on my cousin's ferry at Washington Town on the Brazos River," I explained.

"Cousin?" he asked, growin' suspicious. "Your father comes, too?"

"He's dead," I answered. "I come to settle. Just me. Only relation'd take me in."

He gave me a good look, then seemed to soften. Others were beginnin' to march down the gangplank, and they appeared to interest the Mexicans more. After all, a pale boy with a flour sack full of clothes isn't much of a threat to anybody. I signed my name on some papers and swore I was a good Catholic and had never killed anybody or stolen anythin' worth mentionin'. Then I stepped aside and let the little man have at the Mississippians.

By then Zach was supervisin' the unloadin' of his precious supplies. The packet's crew was as anxious to have done with it as Zach, and they rushed the kegs and sacks and tools down the gangplank and onto the ramshackle wharf. I judged there was close to a wagonful, and I wondered how Zach would ever manage to transport it all home. He knew what to do, though. After payin' the Mexican customs a few silver pieces, he located a freighter and had the supplies driven along the waterfront a way. There they were loaded onto a side-wheel steamer, the *Brazos Queen.*

"Stick close, and put that knife in your belt," Zach advised as he led me away from the steamer. "We don't sail till tomorrow mornin', and we need to find a place to eat and sleep."

"Half the town's inns," I said, pointin' to the signs on the buildin's before us.

"Sure they are," he said, laughin'. "They'd take your money and throw you in a room with a dozen flea-bitten wharf rats for company and nothin' to eat! Mostly grog houses. And worse. Last time I was here a Mexican soldier got himself stabbed and thrown in the Gulf. Same night a freighter's boy had his throat cut, likely for a few coins he was showin' 'round the night before."

"I come from New Orleans, remember?" I told him. "I heard of people murdered before."

"Been one?" he asked with an anxious look in his eyes. "Me neither. Like to keep it that way. How 'bout you?"

I nodded, and he grabbed my hand and led the way past a pack of card-playin' sailors to a side street. We walked on and on till I thought my land-wobblin' legs would collapse. Finally we reached a modest house painted bright yellow with red curtains. Zach knocked at the door, and a sweet-faced girl only slightly older'n myself opened the door and smiled a welcome.

"Afternoon, Miss Sally," Zach said, makin' a sort of bow. "Your mama got a room to let for tonight?"

"More likely she'll want to put you in the barn, Zach Merkins," the girl replied. "Look to need a bath, and this other one's no better."

"We'll wash," Zach promised. "If we get the room."

"We've got a widow downstairs and a pair of horse buyers in back," she said, studyin' me hard. "You can bunk upstairs with Jordy, I guess. If you don't mind his kicking."

"Better'n wharf rats," Zach said, passin' a pair of silver dollars into her outstretched hand. I reached into my pocket, but Zach shook his head. "You're my freight guard, remember?" he added. "Let Papa bear the cost. Likely it'll be the last time I pay your keep."

I couldn't help matchin' his grin. Together we stepped inside. Sally escorted us through the kitchen and along to a small room where her mother did washin'. There was a tub of sudsy water and some linen.

"You can have a wash here," she instructed. "You'll do it, too, Zach Merkins, else I'll not sit you at Mama's table. And this other one, well, see to it he gets at least some of the grit off. The two of you'd pass for goats, I'll wager."

She marched off to busy herself elsewhere, and Zach laughed.

"Doesn't mince words, does she?" I asked. "I never heard the like! I'm all for washin', but Mama worked an inn. She never barked at the guests like that."

"Miz Kelly's got the cleanest place in Galveston," Zach explained as he set his duffle on the floor and peeled off his shirt. "Best eatin', too. What's more, Sally'll give our clothes a scrub. I guess a sharp tongue's to be tolerated. To be real truthful, I don't favor goat smell either."

I laughed as he pointed to the greasy streaks on his bare chest, knowin' I was a fair match. A wash could be downright pleasant, especially if afterward there was a fire to cozy up to. And clean clothes would make a better impression on Cousin J. C.

We'd wriggled out of our clothes and were scrubbin' away with horsehair brushes when a boy about the size of Michael came in to collect our clothes.

"Best hurry," the youngster hinted. "I give you half a shake 'fore Sally chases you out of here and starts scrubbin' your duds. She's partial to chasin' fellows bare naked out to the barn. Does it to me all the time."

"Tim Piper, meet Jordy Kelly," Zach introduced us. "And get to movin'. He ain't jestin'."

The two of us hurriedly concluded our wash and got into such spare clothes as we had. I wore some woolen trousers and a cotton shirt I was fast outgrowin', but Jordy had gone off with my boots, and I was standin' in my stockin' feet when Sally appeared.

"Off with you," she ordered, and Zach led me into the kitchen and along toward the larger common room. We sidled up to the fireplace, gave the widow a nod, and sat beside the hearth. Jordy soon appeared with a platter of cold meat and bread, and we occupied ourselves fillin' our bellies and sharin' news with the horse buyers.

The bread and meats were just a sample of what lay in store for us, though. As night began to fall, Miz Kelly finally appeared. She was a widow herself, and she put me in mind of Mama right away. She was a hair younger maybe, and better at managin' things, but she had the same soft manner. The stew she brewed up close to brought on tears, and the biscuits, all buttered up and laced with honey, were past describin'.

"Jordy says your name's Tim Piper," she said as we finished eatin'. "You're headed up the Brazos with Zach?"

"Yes, ma'am," I answered. "To help my cousin J. C. run the ferry at Washington Town."

"On the La Bahía Road, Mama," Sally explained. "I passed that way last summer visiting Aunt Mary Helen."

"Washington's a new settlement," Miz Kelly added. "I don't often leave Galveston now my husband's passed on. The children sometimes have an excursion, but I've a house to run."

"I understand," I said, smilin'. "My mama worked at an inn in New Orleans. Truth is, we all did."

"That's the way with inns," Miz Kelly said, noddin' to the other guests. "I was in New Orleans once, years ago."

She went on to talk of the visit, recallin' avenues and buildin's that were close to my heart. I couldn't help feelin' a bit homesick for the town, and for the family I'd left behind there. But Miz Kelly spoke of Texas, too, of the pirate Lafitte who'd once lived on Galveston Island and of the dreadful Indians who were troublin' the settlements.

"You mean the Karankawas?" I asked nervously.

"Oh, they're mostly all killed off," Jordy explained. "Were here on the island, you know. They used to eat people."

The widow gasped, and Miz Kelly threw a hard glance at her son.

"Still do as I heard it," I added, starin' at Zach.

"Well, isn't everybody has Mama's biscuits," Sally interceded. "I'd gladly offer 'em a little brother, but they'd find him stringy."

The horse buyers laughed at Jordy's scowl, and for a time the guests joined in a lively discussion of Indian raids. Then Zach remarked on the Mexican customs inspector, and the horse buyers grew agitated.

"I don't see why the government in Mexico City should

collect duties on goods they can't deliver to our farmers themselves," a square-jawed Kentuckian named Plank grumbled. "They don't send soldiers to prevent the Indian raids, and they build no schools or public buildings!"

"They gave us ten years of living with neither taxes nor duties," Miz Kelly argued. "And as good a life as people could ask."

"And now they're takin' it back," Plank complained. "This new El Presidente, Santa Anna, seems eager to send garrisons."

"Not to fight the Indians, though," Zach said, anxiously examinin' the faces around him. "There's a plan to put soldiers in all the towns so the people'll come to heel. If they do it, some folks'll fight."

"Many," Plank agreed.

"Pure foolishness," Miz Kelly declared. "Such talk will bring the Mexican government to send those troops, and they'll be justified in thinking they're needed. I was born in the United States, but between the banks and the land speculators, my father was ruined. We have a good life here under Mexican rule. You know about the goose that laid the golden egg. Don't cut her up, gentlemen. That's my warning!"

FOUR

S<small>ANDWICHED</small> <small>BETWEEN</small> Zach's long, bony body and Jordy's flailin' feet, I thought I'd never get any rest. Gradually the three of us sank into the comfort of Miz Kelly's big feather bed, though, and my mind wandered off in a dream of prowlin' Karankawas and legions of stiff-necked Mexican dragoons. Then daylight seeped in through the window, and Zach shook me awake.

"Steamer's off early," he announced. "No time to waste."

After servin' us a generous breakfast, Miz Kelly packed some food for the trip up the Brazos and bid us good fortune. Sally brought our cleaned clothes, and Jordy appeared with our boots, shinin' like new and feelin' all the better for our feet bein' wrapped in clean stockin's.

I followed Zach to the waterfront somewhat reluctantly. Galveston, for all its rough ways, bore traces of civilization. I worried Washington Town would promise only hard work and peril. The work waited a bit. Peril met us just short of the *Brazos Queen*.

My mind was wanderin' or else I might've seen 'em. Zach, who seemed the reliable sort and sensible to boot, was busy lookin' over the stern of the *Queen*, satisfyin' himself the steamer had his goods aboard and stowed securely. We both had our nerves jarred when we realized we had company.

"Lookee here," a pock-faced lout maybe two years our senior cried as he reached out and threw me against the hard side of a wharf shed. "Got ourselves a pair of likelies this morn."

I blinked my eyes as if to clear my vision. It didn't work. I was starin' up at six boys, most of them not much older nor bigger'n myself. They were ragged and smelled of dead fish. Worse, their eyes spoke of hunger and threatened violence.

"Leave us be!" Zach warned in his sternest voice. "I'll have the soldiers after you."

"Ah, they don't a one of them get up this early," the lout replied, reachin' for Zach's shoulders. Two others groped for his legs, and Zach fell in a heap beside me.

"Let's see what they might be carryin'," one of the younger ones suggested. "Bet they got money. Look to them boots!"

One of the thieves made a grab for my ankle, and I kicked him square in the jaw. He rolled back groanin', and I scrambled to my feet. In an instant I drew my big knife and made a slash for the leader. He leaped back in alarm.

"Lordee, look to that knife!" he cried.

Zach tried to rise, too, but a pair of ruffians jumped atop him and began wrestlin' him to the ground. The leader, meanwhile, tore a plank from a nearby crate and approached me with wild, murderous eyes.

"I got a notion that knife'd look jest fine in my belt," he declared. "After I put it to some use on yer hide, that is."

I took a deep breath, gazed at the encirclin' gang, and swallowed hard. Captain Tom had spun more'n one tale of such a predicament, and I recalled how he said it was important when the odds were long to bite your lip, give a scream, and lash out at anythin' that moves. I gave my best imitation of a crazed Karankawa and made a slash with my knife. The tip of the blade put a neat red stitch in the thigh of the leader, and my hollerin' sent the rest of them to cover.

"What's wrong with him?" one of the younger thieves asked.

"Got dog bit yesterday!" I shouted. "Mad dog bit! I got a hunger for cuttin' up somebody. Oblige me, won't you?"

A couple of them made a rush for me, and I put my blade through one of their arms. The other butted me with his chest, and I rolled back against the shed, hittin' it hard with my head and left shoulder. I didn't lose my grip on the knife, though, and I waved it wildly, sendin' a second rush retreatin'. I then rolled over beside Zach and clouted one of his attackers hard across the back of the skull. Zach tossed the second one off the wharf and into the harbor.

"Want some more?" I screamed, shakin' my head to chase off the pain. "Come ahead and try!"

They'd had enough, though. The leader's leg was near run red with blood, and between my knife and Zach's fists, another one was crawlin' off sobbin'. They shouted a threat or two as they backed away, but they weren't goin' to mess with us no more.

"Lord, Tim, you went plumb crazy!" Zach exclaimed as he helped me to my feet.

"They gone?" I asked.

"Yeah, run back to their rat hole, I'd judge."

"Good," I said, returnin' the knife to my boot and clutchin' my throbbin' head with both hands.

"You're bleedin'," he noted as he helped me over to a

coiled hawser where I could sit down. "Got a pretty lump on that iron head of yours."

"Been bashed before," I said, moanin'.

"Where'd you learn to fight like that?" he asked as he drew a kerchief from his hip pocket and made a bandage of sorts for my head. "New Orleans? Heard they do a lot of knife fightin' down there."

"Only just got the knife," I confessed. "First time I ever swung it at anythin' live."

"Well, you've got a natural talent for it then," he declared. "Yup, and a Texican's way with words as well. Mad dog bit? That's a new one on me!"

"Worked, didn't it?"

"Not so well's the knife did, Tim. Best we grab our sacks and get aboard ship now. I see 'em castin' off the bowlines."

I stumbled along beside him as we stepped to the gangplank and scrambled aboard. The captain took a look at us, grinned, and waved us on toward the cabins.

"See there?" Zach asked as he helped me to a deserted section of deck aft of the paddle wheels. "Even the cap'n can spot a fighter."

"Figure that's what I am?" I asked, managin' a grin.

"Know it," he said, slappin' me on the back. "You saved Papa's money, that's for certain. And maybe my hide. I owe you a debt, Tim Piper. Have to do the same for you one of these times."

I nodded. From what I'd seen of Texas, I didn't doubt he'd have the chance.

Brazos Queen plowed the waters of Galveston Bay with an awkward, sluggish kind of motion. The steamer wallowed somewhat, but she didn't pitch and roll like the packet. My head continued to ache, but for once my stomach didn't betray me. After we passed the little town of San Luis on the mainland and cleared the southern tip of Galveston Island, the *Queen* headed out into the Gulf again, though. It didn't take anytime at all for the deck to start swayin', and I was again at the rail, heavin' up the bits of salt pork and biscuits Miz Kelly'd packed for us.

"I'm never again goin' to sea," I swore as I stretched out on the deck, my head afire.

Zach just laughed, wet a rag, and washed my face.

"Ain't long 'fore we get to Velasco," he assured me. "We got to land some goods there and pick up more passengers. Tomorrow we'll chug on up the Brazos to San Felipe. Then it's along to Washington."

"Two more days?" I cried.

"Can't travel the river at night," he explained. "Too many snags and sandbars. Truth is, not many captains'll do it by day. Better to make the trip by ship than sloshin' through the swamps on horseback, I can tell you!"

I wasn't so sure.

I passed my second night in Texas under a pair of rough cowhides on *Brazos Queen*'s deck, near shiverin' to death from the cold. I'd have gladly taken a berth in a stable if the choice'd been mine, but Zach refused to leave his papa's goods unattended, Velasco bein' a port known for thievin'. As the two of us passed that long, miserable night, beset by swarmin' insects and bitin' winds, Zach talked about his farm and his twin brothers, Amos and Bart, who were but a hair older'n Michael. He had a pair of sisters, too, and three pea-sized brothers.

"Your papa plannin' to populate the country single-handed?" I asked.

"You got a fair-sized family yourself!" Zach barked. "And it takes a lot of hands to work a farm."

Come mornin', Zach started talkin' 'bout Texas. I

didn't know much of the colony's history, and I think Zach enjoyed showin' off how much he did. To start with, he explained how Stephen Austin had brought the first Americans to Texas in '21, landin' in Velasco by schooner. Up to now, close to twenty and a half thousand were said to've come up the Brazos, and more landed elsewhere.

"There was a real battle fought in Velasco back in '32," Zach explained. "All over a cannon some Texicans wanted to haul to Anahuac to attack the customs garrison. Federal colonel name of Ugartechea had a hundred or so men watchin' the customs house in Velasco, and he tried to stop the Texicans sailin' off with the cannon. There were two hundred Texicans, led by a pair of hotheads, Henry Smith and John Austin. Everybody took to shootin' and hollerin', but wasn't much one side could do to ferret out the other. The Federal troops finally ran out of powder and gave it up."

"Doesn't sound like much of a battle," I complained.

"Ten Texicans got kilt, and twenty or so soldiers were shot, some of them bad. Got the government all stirred up, and if ole Stephen Austin hadn't stepped in and settled everybody down, there might've been big trouble."

"I don't see why people are so stirred up," I confessed.

"It's over customs duties and taxes," Zach answered.

"Miz Kelly said it herself, though. Can't expect not to pay duties and taxes, can you? They collect 'em in New Orleans, after all."

"Well, it's true enough, but the taxes go to pay for roads and schools. We got none of that—just garrisons that bully the people and complain we're rebels."

"What would you call it, shootin' at soldiers?" I asked.

"Wasn't but a few followed Smith and John Austin,"

Zach said, scowlin'. "And the government had this army all primed to set off north to punish us."

From what I could figure out, that trouble wasn't altogether dead and buried. Some of the old-timers, people who came out with Stephen Austin in the twenties, had taken up speakin' Spanish and learnin' Mexican law. The latecomers, though, and there were a lot of them, held to the American Constitution and complained of Mexican tyrants. There were lots of quarrels and debates and town meetin's, and more'n a few of the *Queen*'s passengers argued 'bout things on the voyage upriver.

"Looks like I've jumped into a boilin' kettle," I told Zach when we tied up for the night at Austin's town, San Felipe, two-thirds of the way up the Brazos to Washington. "There's some men on the steamer talkin' 'bout fightin' the Mexican army, declarin' independence, or else annexin' Texas to the United States."

"Oh, I wouldn't put much stock in that talk," Zach said, laughin'. "Ain't a one of them men seen the point a Mexican bayonet makes in favor of keepin' the peace."

I nodded in agreement.

"One thing you ought to know 'bout Texicans," Zach added. "They'll take to quarrelin' 'bout anything. And they'll fight for the love of slappin' another man down. Don't make too much of talk or fightin' neither. The country's hard, and it makes folks half crazy, what with summer heat and winter winds that howl like she-devils. You'll find people generally more'n good, though, and most'll welcome you to their door."

I soon had a chance to see that for myself. After passin' one night half frozen on the *Brazos Queen*'s deck, I was delighted when Zach suggested spendin' my third Texas eve under a roof in town. There weren't many inns in the growin' town of San Felipe, for the land thereabouts was mostly settled, and travelers generally took the ole Bexar Trace to the north or the La Bahía Road to Goliad. I'd get well acquainted with 'em both soon enough. Just then, though, I only knew the night was turnin' chill, and I was hungry.

Zach led the way along the river toward the outskirts of town. Most of the houses there were log cabins. Many of them had a room on either side of this gap called a dog run, and the whole thing was covered by a roof. We stopped at one of these dog-run cabins, and Zach knocked on the door.

"What can I do for you, young man?" a kind-faced woman asked as she opened the door. A boy a hair short of Zach stood alongside cradlin' a shotgun. These Texicans, it seemed, weren't all that trustin' of strangers.

"Ma'am, we're bound home from a long journey to New Orleans," Zach explained. "I'm Zach Merkins and this here's Tim Piper. We're cousins. Night's close to froze our joints, and we had some trouble 'long the way. I was hopin' maybe we could pass the night in that shed you got in back and maybe chop some wood for our supper."

"We've not eaten all day," I added, tryin' my best to match Zach's sorrowful look.

"Ah, Ma, look to their boots," the boy said. "Got a shine on 'em. Hasn't the one of them walked much this day, and they look to be able to pay for lodgin'."

"He's right, ma'am," Zach quickly responded. "Only we was robbed. Look to Tim's head there. He's been half gone with fever two days now."

The woman softened, and even the boy seemed impressed by my bloody bandage. She swung the door wide and waved us inside.

"Shed's just for the chickens," she explained as she

pointed to an oak table surrounded by four scruffy youngsters. "Billy there chops what wood we need. Still, if you wouldn't object to some dumplin's and a bite of chicken, I'll share what we got in the pot. You can sleep by the fire with the little ones. I got a quilt in the cupboard'll keep you warm."

"Thank you, ma'am," Zach replied with a grin. I bowed and smiled gratefully. The woman only laughed, muttered somethin' 'bout the charms of Texican menfolk, and headed for the stove. Zach and I discarded our coats, and the boy showed us to a hard bench that we carried to the table.

There wasn't much talk of Mexican customs and taxes in the Phelps house, for such were our benefactors called. Mostly Miz Phelps worried over the wind and whether she'd have a dress finished for some lady in town.

"Ma took up sewin' after Pa got himself Comanche scalped," Billy explained. "Soon I'll be 'prenticed to Mr. Foxton, the blacksmith. Once I learn the trade, I'll look after my family proper."

"Be hard," I said, sighin'. "I lost a papa, too. My mama got herself a new husband, though. Now I'm headed for the ferry at Washington Town, to work for my cousin."

"Thought *he* was your cousin," Billy said, pointin' to Zach.

"I got lots of cousins," I answered. The three of us grinned, and I knew I was found out. Still, Billy never let on, and we passed a peaceful night in San Felipe.

Next mornin' we split some stove wood and patched a gap in the chicken shed to repay the Phelpses' kindness. Afterward we hurried down to the river and climbed aboard the *Queen* 'fore the side-wheeler churned her way upstream. By midafternoon we'd passed a half dozen landin's and two small towns. Just around a bend, where the Navasota River joins the Brazos, Zach pointed excitedly to a cut in the bluff. A small cabin huddled to the bank. Below it lay the ferry.

"You're home, Tim," Zach announced as the steamer slowed. There was a landin' nearby, and the captain announced it as the *Queen*'s final stop.

"Washington Town!" he called. "All prepare to go ashore."

By now there was only a handful of passengers left, but there was considerable freight to be landed. I stood off to one side as the sailors secured the ship to the frail-lookin' plank dock. The others hurried down the gangplank into the arms of waitin' family and friends. I remained a moment with Zach.

"You been good company, Tim," he said, claspin' my hand. "The savin' of me in Galveston, too."

"We'll meet again," I told him. "You said yourself your farm's not far upriver."

"Not many hours in a farmer's day for visitin' friends," he said sadly. "Nor will you have much chance, either. I know J. C., you see."

I frowned. I didn't know J. C. But I knew he was likely down at the ferry or perhaps in that cabin. And there was no time like the present for makin' acquaintances. I waved good-bye to Zach and headed down the gangplank. I was home.

It didn't feel that way, though.

FIVE

I MADE MY WAY PAST the freight handlers and along the shore to the ferry landin'. The cabin was silent, seemingly deserted, but just past it a tall black man stood alongside two great hawsers that were stretched across the river. I approached him cautiously.

"Headed east?" he asked in a boomin' bass voice. "River bein' up, it'll cost you a dollar."

"I don't need to cross," I explained.

"Then best you step aside, young master," the man said. "Be plenty of folks along with a need to use this here ferry."

"But . . ." I objected.

"Stand aside there, boy," a tall, buckskin-clad man called as he led a team of oxen toward the ferry. Behind 'em a long, heavily laden cart plodded along on two great wooden wheels.

"Watch out!" another man shouted. "Get clear, fool boy! Want to get yourself trampled?"

I soon found myself caught between a line of horse-drawn wagons and another of the clumsy ox carts. Steamer passengers also hurried to catch the ferry, for the river, bein' at mid-flood, was unfordable. I reluctantly retreated and let the others grapple for space aboard the ferryboat. Soon the ferryman boomed out, and the first ox cart rolled onto the boat. I turned away and walked along the bank awhile, unsure what to do next. I watched the ferry for a time as it made the slow crossin' from the west to the east bank of the river.

The Brazos current dragged the ferry along its cables, and the powerful ferryman pulled in order to move the ferry toward the far bank. It looked to be exhaustin' work, and I trembled at the notion of puttin' my frail shoulders to the task. At times he had to pull with all his might against the swollen fury of the river, and I easily understood why the rates soared at high water. Then, too, folks didn't have much choice but to use a ferry with the fords flooded.

Three times the ferry crossed the river, each trip exchangin' wagons and passengers headed east from the steamer for others bound westward or eager to travel south on the *Brazos Queen*. I watched with interest the contrast between the newcomers and their woolen trousers and bright dresses and the buckskin-clad frontiersmen. The Texicans seemed rough and as quarrelsome as Zach had warned. Mama would've judged the whole lot in need of a good scrubbin'. But those who passed my way offered a nod or a word in greetin'.

When the ferry made its final journey across to the east bank and back, I ambled past a motley crew of would-be steamer passengers and again met the black man.

"I have a letter from Mr. J. C. Piper," I announced. "I've come all the way from New Orleans, and I—"

"Got no learnin', young master," the ferryman answered. "Cain't read."

"Mister, I—"

"Ain't no mister, neither," he objected. "Name's Jupiter. Folks what care to call me Jupe for short."

He was smilin' friendly enough, and I swallowed my impatience and matched his grin.

"I don't know what to do," I told him. "I've got this letter, and it says—"

"Cain't read that letter," Jupe said, shruggin' his shoulders. "What it say I got to do?"

"Excuse me," a pretty blonde-haired lady said, grippin' the hands of two young daughters securely as she turned back toward us. "Perhaps I can read the letter."

I could've done it myself, but Jupe nodded, and I passed the letter to the lady. As she read Cousin J. C.'s offer, Jupe's grin broadened, and he shook with laughter.

"Why, young master, you could've tole me that you was family," he cried.

"Would have, too, if given the chance," I said, groanin'. "Thank you, ma'am," I told the woman as she passed the letter back into my hands and dragged her children along toward the steamer. She merely nodded and went on. I then asked Jupe, "Can you tell me where my cousin is?"

"Could," he confessed as he tied off the free lines of the ferry. "'Spec' it'd be awright. 'Course, you stick by a minute or so, you're sure to see him yourself. He be along."

Just then I heard a storm of words explode from atop the bluff. A sandy-haired man of about thirty marched down the dusty road, cursin' a pair of horsemen and screamin' at a lead-footed boy who didn't clear the road.

"Young master, that be Mr. Piper now," Jupe said. I gazed at the scarlet-faced man and shuddered. He chewed the end of a cigar and cursed the horsemen a second time. Then he charged past them and grabbed the money box from beside Jupe.

"Hang it all, Jupe!" J. C. shouted. "I told you not to

take these fool Indiana bank notes. I don't get two bits for 'em in Harrisburg or San Felipe, and some aren't worth their ink!"

"Cain't tell 'em one from t'other, Mr. Piper," Jupe answered, hangin' his head. "Don't know my letters."

"Well, it's cost me money this day," J. C. grumbled. "Here's another, and another."

I watched anxiously as my cousin tore the bank notes into shreds and scattered them across the ferry. He was still mutterin' when I finally mustered the courage to hand him the letter.

"What's this?" he asked, starin' at the paper. Then, as he recognized his words, he turned to me, scowlin'. "You?" he bellowed.

"Yes, sir," I said, stiffenin' my spine. "I'm your cousin, Tim Piper, come from New Orleans."

"Lord, you're not half-grown!" he exclaimed. "How tall are you?"

"A hair over five feet," I answered without blinkin'.

"Oh? Figure you can haul yon ferry across to the east bank, do you?"

"I can try," I told him. "And when I try a thing, it generally gets done."

"Does it? And if I told you to get that ferry over and back before dusk?"

"It'd be over and back or I'd be out there sweatin' at it when the sun fell. I'm not big, sir, but you won't find me lackin', either. I been workin' since I could walk at one thing or another, and I never backed away from a challenge."

"I can see that," he noted, pullin' the kerchief from my forehead and havin' a look at the matted hair underneath. "Had a tangle, did you?"

"In Galveston," I explained. "Some wharf rats, as

Zach Merkins calls 'em, tried to rob us. We set 'em on their heels."

"Powerful afeared of you, were they?"

"Of this," I said, drawin' the knife from my boot. "I wasn't the only one bloodied, either."

"I guess not," he said, laughin' as he turned to Jupe. "Well, Jupiter, what do you think? Is he a keeper or do we toss him back?"

"If he know his letters, he can save you some money come collectin'," Jupe answered.

"Do you?" J. C. asked.

"Yes, sir," I told him.

"I see," J. C. declared. "Thin as he is, he'll eat a month's profits, I'll wager." He grabbed my neck and gave me a good shake. I was a bit startled, but I didn't fall. "He's not soft like most city boys. Let's see your hands."

I showed them to him, and he touched the palms with his own rough fingers, then examined my shoulders, my legs, even lifted me up to get a feel for my weight. I felt more like a bag of oats at market than a cousin come to help run a ferry!

"Ain't an easy life here," he finally told me. "We're up early and to bed late. Be all day workin' the ferry, and tendin' folks at the public house by night. That bother you, lookin' after folks?"

"I worked at an inn before," I said. "Mama wrote you that."

"Said you were a stalwart lad, too. But you look to have grit. That'll stand you in fine stead here in Texas. Got any diseases or bad habits I should know 'bout? Been in trouble with the law?"

"I've had measles and the chicken pox," I told him. "Catch a fever sometimes in the winter, and I get seasick on the ocean."

"Not on ferries?" he asked.

"Didn't suffer any comin' up the Brazos on the *Queen*. I'd judge not. As to trouble, I've told a few stories in my time, and I lose my temper. I've pulled some pranks, and you know 'bout my usin' the knife in Galveston. I read the Bible, though, and I write a good hand. I've been told I'm not altogether stupid when it comes to history and cipherin'."

"Jupe?" J. C. asked.

"For a skinny white boy, he looks like he'd be good company," Jupiter answered with a wide grin.

"Help ole Jupe tie down the ferry, Tim. Afterward, come along up the hill to the inn. There are people to meet."

"Yes, sir," I said, stashin' my knife and shakin' his hand. I then turned to help Jupiter secure the ferry, for the sun was beginnin' to fade into the western hills.

When we finished, Jupiter turned toward the cabin and waved me on up the hill.

"Yonder's the public house," he told me. "You go up there now, young master."

"Sure," I said. "Jupe, you suppose you might do me a favor?" I asked.

"That'd depend on the favor," he replied.

"I don't feel much like anybody's master, and I'm not so young as you might think. Fourteen come April. Figure you could call me Tim?"

"Guess that wouldn't cause me to sweat more'n I do already," he said. "You watch out for them young'uns, Tim. They got a talent for mischief."

"I will," I promised as I set off up the hill.

I didn't know much about J. C.'s family, so I couldn't take Jupe's warnin' to heart as I might have otherwise. When I got to the inn, J. C. wasted no time in handin' me a plate of beef and beans, then puttin' me to work totin' fresh water to the four rented rooms and fillin' the kindlin' box beside the kitchen stove. Thereafter I raced around tendin' the needs of the guests. It wasn't till nigh onto bedtime I met J. C.'s pretty, dark-haired wife, Ruth Alice.

"We're delighted to have you with us, Tim," she said, givin' me a sisterly hug and findin' a stick of hard candy for me to chew on. "We've got boarders in all the downstairs rooms just now, so I'm afraid you'll have to share the loft with Titus and Leander."

"Those your boys?" I asked.

"More like worms'n boys," J. C. observed. "They'll try your patience, son, and you're certain to want to use that bowie knife on 'em both. I'd favor you not altogether skinnin' 'em, though, as we've got a fair amount of time invested in their upbringin'."

"I won't," I said, noddin'. "I got brothers, you know. A sister, too. Like as not, I'd feel homesick without a prank or two tried on me."

"Well, don't say you weren't warned," Ruth Alice said. "I'll fetch you some blankets."

"You suppose there's a chance of me havin' some hot water to wash with?" I asked. "Haven't had a chance to scrub since Galveston, and . . ."

"I'll tend to it myself," she said, smilin' approvingly. "Washing's a habit you might pass along to others. It's a thing powerful scarce among Texican menfolk."

"Not healthy, bathin' in winter," J. C. grumbled. "Water's for drinkin', after all. What's not caught in the cisterns has to be carried up from the river. Poor use of labor draggin' wash water uphill."

"Wasn't meanin' to soak in a tub," I explained. "Just wash with a rag."

"You do either, just as you like," Ruth Alice told me. "Just as you like, Tim. And afterward I'll have a look at that lump on your head. It appears to want draining."

"Fancies herself a doctor, you know," J. C. whispered. "I wouldn't let her within ten feet of me with a knife."

I laughed at the jest, then carried my knapsack back into the common room and climbed the ladder leadin' to the loft. I wasted no time sheddin' my clothes and pullin' on a nightshirt.

"You Tim?" a straw-haired boy of about ten asked as I prepared to return to the kitchen for my wash.

"Sure am," I answered. "Your cousin."

"I'm Leander," the boy explained. "Titus there's asleep. He's just a little 'un. Figure to stay?"

"No place else to go," I told them. "You watch over my sack, will you? Hate for the snake to get out."

"Snake?" Leander asked.

"Rattler. Caught him down by the river. Thought I'd milk him in the mornin' 'fore I skin him. Snakes make good belts, you know."

"He still alive?" the boy cried. "A rattler? Here?"

"Oh, I got him tied proper," I said, fightin' to keep a straight face. "Hasn't a snake gotten loose of my knots since the one back in Natchez."

"One got loose?"

"Bit a groom over at the colonel's stable. Killed him. Later on I found out my brother Michael went and messed with my pack, let that snake loose. Lucky Michael takes baths. Snakes don't like soap, so that rattler didn't bite Mike. Otherwise, I'd be missin' a brother sure."

"I'll watch your stuff," Leander promised. "'Course Titus might be curious."

"Am not," the younger boy said, sittin' up. "Not where snakes's involved."

"Well, it's smart," I told them. "Be back along later. We'll get acquainted proper tomorrow."

They nodded solemnly. I could tell the snake story had put them in awe of me, though, and surely spoiled a fine prank.

"Just as well," Ruth Alice told me when I shared the tale in the kitchen. "Won't hurt those two to have somebody salt their tails for once. Terrors of the Brazos bottoms, the both of them!"

"Well, a boy's just bound to break loose of the reins now and then," I declared. "In the blood, Mama says."

She laughed, then drew a kettle of steamin' water off the stove for my wash.

"I'll be along in a half hour to clear away things," she explained as she opened the door. "Meanwhile, you've the kitchen to yourself."

"Thanks," I told her.

"Man's due his privacy, after all."

A man? I thought. It sounded just fine. As for privacy, it was somethin' rarely come by in a family of eight. Texas was lookin' better every moment.

SIX

It was good I got some rest that first night at the ferry. I
didn't have a chance to so much as catch my breath
thereafter for better'n a week. Most of that time I was
occupied with Jupe down at the ferry, helpin' him pull
that raftlike platform across the surgin' Brazos. The
ferry, I soon learned, was the Brazos crossin' for the old
La Bahía Road, connectin' East Texas with the mission
town of Goliad and beyond that Matamoros and Saltillo.
It was a rare day when a dozen or so travelers didn't pass
our way, and with the river up, we did good business.

I quickly caught on to the ins and outs of the ferry
business. I discounted paper money. Those bills that
looked suspicious, especially the American bank notes
J. C. mistrusted, I refused entirely. Mostly we took U.S.
coins and Mexican silver, when we weren't offered
chickens or eggs or cider instead. Often a frontiersman
would bring in a fresh-killed buck or a fine hide to pay
his passage and pick up a bit of change besides. The
boarders were partial to fresh meat, and aside from what
Leander, Titus, and I could fish from the river or J. C.
could shoot on his rare hunts in the Brazos bottoms, we
were powerful short of that commodity.

As to the boys, I wasn't able to hold 'em at bay long
with the snake tale. They vexed me considerably. One

mornin' I found sap in my trousers. Come midday, Titus brought me a bowl of soup full of little green chili peppers that set my mouth afire. Then, as I trudged up the hill with arms half out of their sockets from tuggin' at the ferry lines, they ambushed me with horse dung.

Enough was enough! When they were fast asleep, I slipped up on 'em, bound and gagged 'em, opened wide the loft window, and dragged 'em bed and all out onto the roof. They passed the whole night out there in their nightshirts, and I warned 'em to expect like treatment if they didn't come to terms. It was as good as a declaration of war, or, as Jupe said, wavin' a red sheet in the face of some Mexican bull!

They counterattacked when I was washin'. There I was, skin naked, and they raced in, grabbed every last stitch of my clothes, and escaped into the common room, gagglin' like a couple of magpies. I was fixed good and proper, for I couldn't very well chase 'em barebottomed, and I was sure to freeze if I stood around forever with nothin' but a damp rag for cover.

"Lord, what'd I do to deserve such mistreatment?" I asked, knowin' for certain how ole Job must've felt. Then, just when I was about to set off after 'em naked or not, Ruth Alice knocked at the door, handed in a fresh shirt and a pair of trousers, and soon as I was decent, appeared with a boy's ear in each of her hands.

"Got something to say, do you, boys?" she asked.

"Sorry, Tim," Titus said, wincin' as his mother tightened her grip. "Mama says we gone too far and are sure to suffer for it."

"I am already," Leander said, howlin'. "Didn't mean to . . . well, that's not true. We did mean to steal your clothes, Tim, but it was just in fun."

"Won't happen again, will it?" Ruth Alice asked.

"No, Mama," Leander promised. "One switchin's enough."

"More'n enough," Titus agreed, rubbin' his bottom as he fought to free his ear.

"I wouldn't interfere with your business, Tim," she told me, "but these little devils know better than to disturb our boarders by such doings. I thought perhaps you'd like to show them how to wash up before going to bed. Care to take charge?"

"Yes, ma'am," I said, grinnin'.

"I'll be waiting outside if you need any help," she said, more to the boys than to me. "Armed," she added, handin' over one child at a time and then reappearin' momentarily in the doorway, switch in hand.

It was a sight to see, those two shiverin' away as they washed themselves with cold water. All the time there I was, sittin' atop their bundled clothes and eyein' the back door.

"You wouldn't leave us stark naked in here with the fire nigh out, would you?" Titus asked.

"Depends," I answered. "Time to make a truce, do you figure?"

"We get our clothes back?" Leander asked.

"If you promise to put an end to our war. Well?"

"Truce," Leander reluctantly pledged.

"Truce," Titus echoed.

With our war at an end, I confess I slept a bit easier in the loft. Later on, when a few boarders went on their way, I had a bed downstairs. Those days sharin' a bed with gamey buckskinners and tobacco-chewin' teamsters made that night on the deck of *Brazos Queen* seem downright paradise. I soon found the soft rustlin' of

Leander and Titus preferable to the noisy snorin' and occasional mumblin's of the boarders. Thereafter I stuck to loft livin'.

Another trial was gettin' acquainted with the family dogs. There were four of them—Brown Dog, Spot Dog, Black Dog, and White Foot Dog. I had a notion Titus and Leander'd named the lot of them, and I suspected the boys had put those beasts onto my scent from the first day. If they weren't chewin' my trousers, they were bitin' my legs. And it was nigh impossible to eat beef and biscuits without 'em makin' off with half your meal.

They didn't bother Jupe.

"Jest give 'em a good kick and be done wid 'em," he advised. "Elsewise you find 'em some meat and make yourself friends. By and by that black 'un's goin' to eat you, Tim Piper. He fancy you, I think."

Not bein' too long-legged and short of the heart for kickin' dogs, I made me some rabbit snares and soon had fresh meat enough to offer those dogs some.

The next challenge to life and limb came upon me quite sudden and purely by chance. Jupe and I were tuggin' the ferry lines and bringin' her across to the west bank toward the end of March when somethin' moved in the water right beside Jupe's foot. I didn't notice right away, but he let go the line and skipped away, hollerin' to high heaven. I saw what it was then. A long, brownish-colored snake with a whitish mouth was aboard the ferry.

"Moc'sin!" Jupe cried.

I knew a cottonmouth when I saw one, and that snake sure fit the mold. There it was, mouth openin' up as if to swallow a turkey, and me all that stood between Jupe and glory. I drew out my knife, stomped my foot on that snake's middle, and neatly sliced off his head.

"Lord Almighty!" a woman passenger screamed as I tossed the snake's head into the river.

"Tim!" Jupe yelled.

Only then did I realize we'd both let go the lines. The river took charge of the ferry and gave her a good shake. 'Fore Jupe could get the lines straightened out, the fool ferry shuddered and hopped in the current, knockin' me right off the edge and into the river.

"Help!" I cried as I floundered in the chill water. "Jupe?"

He was occupied with the ferry, though, and all he could do was stare helplessly while the current carried me downstream. I flailed at the water and screamed with all my heart, knowin' those sounds were sure to be my last. I was drowned sure!

Fate's a trickster, they say. For just as my head dipped beneath the surface for what was certain to be the last time, somethin' grabbed my arm and pulled me toward shore. I blinked the water from my eyes and did my best to kick along with my rescuer. Would you believe it? Black Dog had jumped in and was tuggin' me to shore!

The big beast got me to the shallows and left me to crawl the rest of the way myself. He stood on the sandy bank, barkin' as if to scold me for not knowin' better'n to get myself drowned. Then Titus and Leander ran over and joined in the fracas.

"Cain't you swim, Timmy?" Titus asked. "Why, any fool knows better'n to jump in a river if'n he cain't swim!"

"He goin' to learn!" Jupiter shouted as he charged between the two boys, nudged Black Dog out of the way, and picked me up bodily. "Boy saves my life cuttin' a snake in two, then goes and gets himself throwed in the river! You drown, I got all the work to myself again. What call you got to do that, Tim Piper? Eh?"

"Didn't plan it," I said, tremblin' from the suddenness of it all. "Always figured to learn to swim. I dog paddled some back at Natchez, but I never had the time later."

"You got it now," Jupe said, draggin' me upriver. When he was satisfied all the passengers had disembarked from the ferry, he kicked off his shoes, discarded his ragged cotton shirt, and peeled me down to my drawers.

"What in heaven's name you goin' to do with me, Jupe?" I cried.

"Goin' to see you know how to swim," he said as he dragged me into the river and left me to flounder in water just over my head.

"Don't go to splashin' like a baby!" he yelled. "Kick with them feet. Now use your hands. Better. That's a dog paddle, all right. Keep you up a minute or so. Now you reach out and pull that water to you."

I immediately managed to plunge headfirst toward the bottom, and he dove down and fetched me.

"Ain't so easy's I thought!" he barked as I sputtered and coughed. "But we get it done. You see if we don't."

And we did, too. I near drowned myself three more times, but in the end I could struggle ten or fifteen yards without dippin' 'neath the surface, and I knew I'd soon be able to cross the river from bank to bank.

The first of April Zach Merkins paid me a visit. He'd been busy readyin' his fields for spring plantin', but he'd come down to the river to do a bit of huntin', and J. C., after stompin' and shoutin' some, gave me half the mornin' off to join in.

"You gone and growed some," Zach noted as he showed off his gun, an old fowlin' piece he called a chicken gun.

"Got some taller yourself," I told him.

"Sure," he replied. "Got a fair bit of chin whiskers, and my mustache is comin' in fair."

I had to look hard to see either, but they were there, all right. I tried not to let my envy show, but his grin told me I wasn't altogether successful.

"You've yet to turn fourteen," he told me. "I didn't have much whiskers myself back then."

Back then? Wasn't all that long ago. But I kept my tongue and followed him into the tangle of briars and scrub cedar that led to the taller oak forest. If it'd been up to me, I'd brought along one of the dogs to scare up a bobwhite or two, but it turned out Zach was after bigger game. He pointed to a line of tracks in the sandy soil, and I smiled. I wasn't much of a frontiersman, but I knew deer tracks when I saw 'em.

We were maybe half an hour stalkin' that deer. I didn't do much save follow quietly, watchin' what Zach did. He was a hunter, all right, and he took great care to keep the wind on his face so the deer wouldn't pick up our smells. We kept low, too, so as not to show more'n a shadow of ourselves. Then, finally, we come upon the deer—three of 'em.

"Stay here," Zach whispered. "I got to go in, get close. This fool gun won't carry buckshot far."

I nodded my understandin' and watched with admiration as he sneaked up on the deer. He was a rare wonder of a stalker, I decided, for he got within about ten feet 'fore startlin' the deer. The first two raced off in a flash. The third started, but Zach fired his piece, and a blast of shot drove the deer to the ground.

"You got him!" I shouted as the powder smoke cleared.

"Yeah," Zach mumbled as he stepped to the deer and drew out his knife. He cut the fallen creature's throat, then lifted the carcass so the blood'd drain. I swallowed hard and looked away a moment.

"I'll ask J. C. if maybe I can borrow his rifle and try my hand next time," I said as Zach began the skinnin'. "Figure you can teach me to sneak up on 'em that way?"

"Don't need to with a real rifle, Tim. I plan to get me one soon. Jubal Parker's gone to New Orleans to bring out some new guns and a wagonload of powder. Papa's paid him for two rifles, one for him and one for me."

" 'Fore you even get your harvest in?" I asked.

"Been talk of trouble lately," he explained.

"Indians?"

"That and others. Hard feelin's over taxes. Some heavy-handed soldiers come by, too, checkin' on land titles. It's even worse in East Texas. I heard tales of families thrown off their own land, run out of their cabins, all on account of some fools in Saltillo not recordin' deeds proper."

"That won't make much difference to us, will it?"

"Likely not," he confessed. "Still, Papa likes to be ready."

"It's a good way," I admitted.

SEVEN

I TURNED FOURTEEN April 21. In my two months at the ferry, I'd yet to see Washington Town itself, and J. C. decided my birthday was the proper moment to show me the town. I expected the place to be a smaller version of Galveston, or at least as big a place as San Felipe or Velasco. When I marched past the warehouses and corrals J. C. co-owned with Mr. John Lott and continued along into the town proper, I couldn't help feelin' disappointed. There wasn't but one real street, which was the La Bahía Road. In Washington folks called it Ferry Street. On either side of the dusty trail were a dozen or so plank and log-walled buildin's. There were three stores, a pool hall and grocery, two taverns, and Miz Mann's boardin' house. Samuel Heath had a blacksmith shop on the eastern edge of town, and Mr. Noah Byars operated a gun shop on the west end. Four doctors had houses in Washington, and we did a fair amount of business ferryin' patients across the Brazos.

As we made our way from one place to the next, it soon became clear that J. C. was doin' more'n just introducin' folks to his cousin. He was showin' me off!

"Come out from New Orleans, did he?" Mr. Byars, the gunsmith, asked. "Well, it's fittin'. This is a young country, and it'll need men to grow."

Mr. Lott, who operated a tavern in town besides ware-houses and corrals, offered me a mug of strong cider and toasted my birthday.

"You ever get tired of this cousin of yours hollerin', come see me, Tim boy," he said as I tried to get the fiery liquid down my throat. "I can use a sober man workin' for me."

I deemed Washington a fiercely friendly place. Oh, there were a few jests sent my way, too, but I saw through 'em easy enough.

"Texas is a country of newcomers," J. C. told me as we headed back to the public house. "Guess you'd say we naturally welcome new arrivals."

"I been here more'n two months," I reminded him.

"Well, you got to wait a bit to see if a fellow's goin' to stay."

"Figure I will, do you?"

"You outlasted Leander and Titus, didn't you? Couldn't drown you in the river. I expect you'll last."

He laughed and rested a hand on my shoulder, and I guessed he wasn't altogether sorry I'd come west.

J. C. and Ruth Alice did my birthday up right. She cooked big fat pork chops and stewed some yams. To top everythin' off, she baked a pie usin' some stowed-away peaches. Afterward Ruth Alice presented me with a new cotton shirt she'd got me at Mr. Ayres's store, and J. C. produced a pair of moccasins he'd made from a cowhide. Leander and Titus saved their gift for last, and I couldn't've been more surprised! With their papa's help, they'd made me a regular bed! It had oak sides and a straw mattress that rested on stretched ropes. The marvel of it was how they carried the thing up to the loft without my takin' note.

Zach happened by a bit later, while the whole bunch of us were in the common room singin' with the boarders. He'd made me a buckskin jacket from his deerhide, and I believe sportin' that coat and my new mocs, I was a passable Texican.

"You'll do," Zach declared, "though you do seem a bit of a runt to me."

"Well, you're not so much yourself!" I barked. "Jupe says I'm as good a hand as he's known at the ferry. You got to admit I'm gettin' strong."

He felt my shoulders and laughed. Boilin' mad, I grabbed him and did my best to wrestle him to the ground. It was a mistake, for he was half again my size and farm strong. I wound up with a mouthful of dirt and a whack to the seat of my pants.

"Don't take yourself so serious, Tim Piper," he advised. "And be more careful of who you take for a wrestlin' partner."

Zach left shortly, for it was a fair walk back to his farm, and I sat on the porch of the house, gazin' off at the river. It put me in mind of Natchez, and I was suddenly overcome with homesickness. I hadn't even had a letter from Mama, nor a word of Michael, Agnes Elizabeth, or the little ones. Letters were slow gettin' to Texas, I knew, but you'd have thought they'd remember my birthday.

"Feeling sad?" Ruth Alice asked as she stepped through the door and sat down at my side.

"A little homesick," I confessed. "I never had a birthday without Mama and my sister and brothers around 'fore this year."

"You think maybe I could give you a hug for her?"

"Guess so," I said, gazin' up into her smilin' eyes. She gave me the hug, then followed my eyes out to the river.

"It's strange how even in the evening, with only a sliver of moonlight out, you can see the outline of the river down there."

"Hear it, too," I noted, listenin' to the croakin' of the frogs and the chirpin' of the crickets. "There's a cardinal singin' tonight."

"Spring's a season for birds," she declared. "Time for growing things. The garden will be bringing up fresh greens soon. They'll be welcome."

"You and J. C. been in Texas long?" I asked.

"Ten years," she told me. "Came out just after Leander was born. J. C.'s father had brought some horses down from Kentucky to sell, and he fell in love with the country. He had an eye for possibilities, Daddy Piper. Once he got the ferry going, though, he didn't have time to operate it proper. Sent for J. C. Daddy moved on, but we stayed on."

"You bring Jupe?" I asked.

"He was Daddy Piper's," she said, turnin' to where a light curl of gray smoke rose from the cabin's chimney. "I suppose you could say Jupiter came with the ferry. Slavery's not legal in Mexico, you know, so we bonded Jupe as a servant."

"He can't leave, though, can he?" I asked.

"No," she admitted. "I suppose it's the same thing as slavery, really. I listen to him singing his spirituals in the mornings, or on Sundays, when we quit work early. It tears at me, keeping a man like a horse, to do my bidding. I wasn't raised Southern, you see. J. C. met me in Ohio."

"I didn't know," I told her. "You don't sound Texas, but you haven't got a Yankee tongue, either."

She laughed and shook her head.

"I wonder if he minds much, ole Jupe," I said then.

"Don't know," she whispered. "He doesn't talk much. Just keeps to himself."

"Yeah," I said, sighin'.

"Sure seems lonely sometimes," I said, pointin' to where Jupe sat a hundred yards off, starin' eastward across the Brazos.

"I guess maybe he is," Ruth Alice observed. "He stays in that little cabin all by himself, and if he shares five words with anyone, it's news to me."

I'd done my fair share of wonderin' 'bout Jupe, especially after he took charge of my swimmin', and I suppose I'd been lonely often enough to spot the symptoms.

"Go ahead," Ruth Alice suggested, wavin' toward Jupe. "I don't imagine he'd begrudge you a few words on your birthday."

"Maybe not," I mumbled as I set off down the hillside.

Jupe was no spendthrift when it came to words, but his face pretty much let you know where he stood on things. When I greeted him, he motioned me over and managed half a smile.

"Fair night for watchin' the river," I told him. "Or thinkin'."

"Fair," he agreed.

"How come you figure J. C. to make such a fuss over a birthday?" I asked. "'Specially when he hollers half the day at some teamster or lodger. Gets downright calm 'round me."

"'Cause you're family," Jupe declared. "Man gets that way, particular 'round boy children. Takes pride in 'em."

"Was your papa like that, Jupe?"

"Oh, that was long ago," he muttered. "Back Alabama way."

"But you remember it, don't you?" I asked.

"Oh, I got no head for recollectin'," Jupe said, laughin' nervously.

"Sure, you'd remember that," I argued. "Lord, Jupe, it's just me's all. You can tell Tim Piper anythin' and know he'll keep it to himself. Who'd go and want to listen to me even if I had a thing worth tellin'? I told you 'bout my papa, and about Cap'n Tom, too."

"Ain't much to recall," he explained. "Only a hazy picture of a man. That's how it is with slave boys, Tim Piper. You'd know that from your days on the big river."

"Never thought on it, Jupe."

"Slave's got no real family," Jupe said sadly. "Not me anyhow. Just them that owns him."

"Like J. C.'s daddy."

"Fair enough man, Mr. Piper, by most accounts. Bought me out of hard times. Never lashed me. Still, there was Lucille and young Hadrian."

"Who?"

"My woman and boy," he said, frownin'. "Hadrian'd be your age, bit bigger now maybe."

"And you had to leave 'em behind?"

"Slave's just somethin' a plantation man buys and sells, you see. Like cane sugar or plow blades."

"You must miss 'em. I miss Mama, my sister, and my brothers."

"Passes after a time, them feelin's."

I shook my head, not believin' a word of it.

"Ruth Alice says the Mexicans don't hold with slave-holdin'," I said. "So you're not a—"

"I put my mark on a paper," Jupe explained. "Bonds, they call it. I work some years and I'm a free man. But it's not so different."

"It's not?"

"Where'd I go? What'd I do? Ain't nothin' but a long

path of weariness to march down. I got my cabin and what solitude I can come by. Stands me better'n most."

"You could leave easy enough. I hear there's country north of here a man could lose himself in easy."

"Man runs, there's those who'll hunt him," Jupe explained. "And if I got away, there'd be Indians out that way. Besides, I couldn't abide the quiet. Hereabouts I got you to jabber at me all the day. Titus and Leander got to prank somebody, and I be handy. Mr. and Miz Piper be fair folk, after all."

"Sure," I said, settlin' in beside him. We stared silently toward the river rollin' past, each of us rememberin' faces now far away. But there was space between us, too. After all, I could step aboard *Brazos Queen* if I had the fare. Jupe couldn't. And the more I thought about his Lucille and young Hadrian, the more I got to missin' my own family.

I wrote Mama a long letter that next day, tellin' her about the buckskin jacket, the peach pie, and all. J. C. sent it with a fellow bound downriver who promised to post it at Velasco. Each day thereafter I hoped an answer would arrive, but no news came. At least no news from New Orleans.

That summer considerable ruckus was raised down on the coast. An Alabama lawyer name of Buck Travis took it in his head to go after the soldiers at Anahuac. There were about fifty of them, led by a certain Captain Tenorio, and they didn't put up a fight.

"No, they marched back to Bexar real peaceful," Zach told me. "But they won't stay that way."

He was right, too. Word out of Bexar, which was called San Antonio by some, had the garrison there up in arms. Worse, the Mexican president, Santa Anna, had sent his brother-in-law, General Cos, to Matamoros on the Gulf with a fair-sized army. El Presidente wasn't any too tolerant of rebels, and he was said to've told this General Cos fellow to find the rebels and hang 'em quick.

From the talk I heard among J. C.'s boarders, most of the Texicans were for supplyin' the rope.

"Travis is a blamed fool," one of them said. "We've been through all this before. These garrisons don't bother us. As long as they've enough to eat and drink, they look after themselves. As to customs, they deserve to be paid. I'll wager it's smugglers behind the whole thing."

"Now they've brought a whole army marchin' down on us!" another spoke up. "How's that to set with 'em? I'll bet Travis and his crew skedaddle across the Sabine and leave us to deal with Cos and his battalions."

"He's a dangerous idiot!" J. C. hollered. "Doesn't he know Santa Anna's just put down rebellions in Zacatecas and Coahuila!"

Well, I didn't even know where those places were, but one of the boarders did. He told a grim tale of how Santa Anna captured five thousand rebels at that Zacatecas place and shot the whole bunch of them. Now the same soldiers were headed across the Rio Bravo toward Bexar and thence toward me! The docks of Galveston were startin' to sound downright peaceable.

Most of Texas must've felt the same because it wasn't long 'fore towns started sendin' General Cos letters pledgin' loyalty and callin' Travis and his gang a pack of drunkards who didn't represent the true feelin's of Texas. Cos brought his army along to Bexar, across country with scant water in the hottest time of the year, and the discomforts of the journey seemed to settle him down some. He finally bedded down his army in Bexar and sent out word he'd be satisfied if Travis and some other culprits were turned over for trial.

"Trial?" Zach asked as we set off huntin' in late August. "Some trial! Be shot, the whole bunch of them. And half the folks on that list, as I hear it, are Mexican supporters of the legal Constitution of 1824 like Lorenzo de Zavala."

"So what's to happen?" I asked.

"Well, I don't know for certain," Zach confessed, "but I'll be hanged if I see good people turned over to a Mexican tyrant and shot down like dogs!"

I just shrugged my shoulders. I didn't know this de Zavala or much of anybody else, and it seemed to me this general might not be one to argue with. Cos had the whole of Texas stirred up, though, and people willin' to hang Travis themselves a few months back were cleanin' their rifles and promisin' trouble if ole Cos stepped north of Bexar.

I put it all down to the quarrelsome nature of Texicans and busied myself with my work. There was plenty of it, too. When I wasn't helpin' Jupe at the ferry, J. C. had me pickin' fruit or helpin' some neighbor with harvest. There was work millin' corn, too, and it put a few coins in my pocket. I saved up most of this money, hopin' I might buy a chicken gun so I could hunt deer and javelinas like Zach. Instead I had to satisfy myself with snarin' rabbits or catchin' fish.

A little of the money I spent sendin' letters to New Orleans by way of *Brazos Queen*. The captain promised to put my writin's aboard a New Orleans packet, and I was satisfied they'd reach Captain Tom from there. Everybody along the waterfront knew Tom Fitzgerald, after all.

My investment paid off, for in September, the steamer pulled up at high water with a package for me. Inside was a letter from Mama.

"My, how relieved we were to finally hear from you," she wrote. "Many nights we've prayed our beloved Tim wasn't shipwrecked or scalped by wild Indians."

"All those letters!" I cried. "Nary a one reached 'em!"

She sent me two shirts and a sketch of my brothers and sister done by a student artist. It wasn't real good, but I could tell Michael was growin' tall, and Agnes Elizabeth hadn't lost her charms.

I was in a mood to climb clouds, and I hurried to write an answer and dispatch it with the *Queen* 'fore it sailed back to Galveston.

Mama'd written about the trouble in Mexico. Folks were raisin' money in New Orleans, it appeared, and talkin' of a war to liberate Texas. So far as I could see, we didn't need liberatin', but when I showed that part of the letter to J. C., he judged we might need friends in time.

"You hear dark rumors comin' out of Mexico City," he told me. "New taxes and hard laws. Those that raise their voices in argument are jailed. Stephen Austin just got back to San Felipe after better'n a year locked up in a dungeon! A more sensible, peace-lovin' gentleman never walked the earth! I don't favor the smell of things."

I nodded solemnly and vowed to find out more. J. C. wouldn't talk about it around Ruth Alice, though, and whenever I raised the matter with Jupe, he just shook his head.

"I don't worry myself over what I got no say about," he told me. "I pull dis ferry and mind my own self. Best you do the same, Tim Piper."

Zach, on the other hand, could always be depended on

for a few words one way or another. We were out huntin' javelinas, a kind of wild pig with tusks, and I brought up ole Santa Anna.

"Say El Presidente was a javelina," he suggested. "Makes a fair comparison, you know. Santa Anna runs around like he's mad at everybody, and he'd as soon tusk you as give you the time of day. Only way to stop him's sharpen a stick and run it into his gut."

The trouble with that, as we found out, was that it didn't always work. The two of us were straddlin' a javelina run—a sort of path they tore through the brush. We heard one comin', and we got our sticks down low. Then, just as the pig came tearin' down the trail one way, the big mama javelina of all tarnation roared down on us from the backside. I speared the first one, and Zach took a try at the second. He missed, and that big pig was gruntin' and wavin' its tusks around, and pretty soon the both of us was scramblin' up the branches of this big live oak, feared for our lives.

"Yup, it's a problem," Zach said, scratchin' his head. "You miss with a javelina or El Presidente, either one, you're up a tree."

"Difference is a bunch of bayonets'd be waitin' 'stead of one fool pig."

"Right now that pig looks like it's enough," Zach replied.

We were up there better'n an hour waitin' for the javelina to move along. Zach spent the whole time tellin' 'bout Santa Anna fightin' this bunch of revolutionists or that, callin' himself Napoleon of the West, and hangin' a hundred medals on his jacket.

"Thinks himself a genius," Zach declared.

"Maybe he is," I suggested.

"You know who the real Napoleon was?" he asked.

I did, for in New Orleans he's remembered for sellin' the whole of Louisiana to Thomas Jefferson.

"Guess that wasn't such a genius thing to do, was it?" Zach asked. "And in the end, the British whipped him bad at Waterloo. The British! Why, my grandpa beat those same redcoats with Andy Jackson at New Orleans! So Napoleon maybe wasn't so much after all."

"Conquered most of the world," I noted. "Lot more'n Texas."

EIGHT

As the oak trees along the river took on their autumn coats of gold and scarlet, I couldn't help noticin' a change in the folks around me. Even the old-timers spoke more and more of Texas as apart from Mexico, and almost nobody thought the current trouble would pass without things comin' to a head. Mr. Byars was kept busy repairin' rifles and pistols, and we hauled more powder and lead across the Brazos than horseshoe iron and cookin' pots.

People began to speak of war, of defendin' our rights like our grandpas had done at Lexington and Trenton and Yorktown. There were old-timers aplenty about who'd fought the Creeks with Andy Jackson and later shot up the British at New Orleans. Some organized little companies of their neighbors and took to marchin' 'round like militia.

"We aim to be ready in case there's Indian trouble," Zach told me when he took his place among 'em. I noticed nobody was lookin' north toward the Cherokees and Comanches, though. They were gazin' southwest— at Bexar and General Cos.

I had a longin' to join the men in their mock battles, but bein' small and armed with but a knife, my offer to serve was met with laughter.

"Plan to run up to ole Cos and cut off his mustache, Timmy?" Mr. Lott cried. "You keep those supplies movin' across the river, son. That's the highest kind of service. We need powder more'n men just now."

Maybe it was true, and maybe it wasn't. Only thing I knew was I had to tug at the ferry lines all day while Zach and the others played soldier.

"Feelings are runnin' high," J. C. explained when we washed up for supper one night. "The war camp had a fair-sized number of hotheads all along. But when Stephen Austin came back from Mexico and told how he'd been thrown in prison for months on end with never so much as a charge laid against him, well, that set others to thinkin'."

A day or two later one of the boarders read from the newspaper they started printin' in San Felipe.

"War is our only recourse. There is no other remedy. We must defend our rights, ourselves, and our country by force of arms."

Stephen Austin said that. His was a voice to urge caution, to argue compromise. Now nobody had much doubt there'd be fightin'.

It started the second day of October, in a little town called Gonzales, close to Bexar. The people there had a cannon given 'em to fight off Indians, and General Cos, notin' the temperament of the people, sent some cavalry down to fetch it. The people went and buried their cannon. When reinforcements arrived with orders to take the cannon by force, the Gonzales militia dug up their cannon, mounted it on an ox cart, and formed a line of battle across a river.

"Wasn't much of a fight, as I hear," Zach told me. "Nobody wants war just now. There's harvestin' yet to be finished, and crops to get to market. We don't sell our cotton and corn, there won't be cash for powder or rifles."

But the Gonzales folks had made their point. Texicans weren't goin' to stand by and have their rights trampled. And if they didn't actually defeat any Mexican army, neither did they surrender their cannon. General Cos knew he had a fight on his hands.

Down at San Felipe, delegates from all over Texas met to have what they called a consultation or convention. J. C. said that meant everybody was goin' to speak his mind.

"Fool hotheads'll talk of blood and war and glory," he complained. "Others'll argue and mutter about the cost of powder and the consequences. Nothin' good can come of so many speech makers gatherin' together!"

I didn't know whether anythin' good came of the speeches or not. But as I helped Jupe load cotton bales and cornmeal sacks and pull the ferry across the Brazos, I noticed the grim faces of the buckskin-clad men and boys marchin' to San Felipe.

"They're so young," Ruth Alice said with a sigh as she ladled out stew for the would-be soldiers stayin' the night at our public house. "Two are scarcely over fourteen."

"I'm fourteen myself," I remarked.

"I know," she said. "Too young by half."

I didn't feel young, though. My arms and shoulders were splittin' out my shirt stitchin', and my legs were long and lean from walkin' the bottoms with Zach.

"Got chin whiskers now, Tim," Zach pointed out after we impaled a javelina on our sticks the second week of November. "Won't be long 'fore you're a soldier your own self."

"I don't have a gun," I said, sighin'.

"Maybe I'll bring you one back from Bexar."

"From Bexar?" I asked, confused.

"Yeah, looks to me as if you'll have these sharp-toothed pigs to yourself a time. There's an army formin' up to march on Bexar and chase General Cos clear of Texas. Ole Ned Burleson, a famed Indian fighter, is takin' command. He's called for soldiers. I got nothin' else to do till plantin', so I'm off to be a soldier."

"You make a big target," I grumbled. "Gone crazy growin', Zach."

"Oh, I never knew a Mexican soldier to hit anythin'," he assured me. "It's those bayonets I aim to stay clear of."

"You do that. I don't have so many friends hereabouts that I can stand to lose one."

"Don't plan to get lost," he said, grinnin'. "Nor shot, either."

The next mornin' I excused myself from ferryin' for the first time since I got to Washington. Jupe looked up in surprise, then nodded sadly as he saw me head to where Zach and a half dozen others were formin' into a line to march south. I walked with 'em half a mile, listenin' to their boasts 'bout shooin' Mexicans like flies and sendin' the Napoleon of the West runnin' for cover. There was a hint of worry in the older ones' eyes, though, and I fretted some that Zach would get himself kilt.

"Wish I'd known he was goin'," Jupe said when I returned to the ferry. "I got a wishbone charm I'd give him to keep him safe and a good mad stone to take off fever."

"Maybe he won't need 'em," I said, pickin' up one end of a steamer trunk while he lifted the other. "These Texicans are big on talk."

"Look yonder," Jupe said, pointin' to a gang of riflemen gatherin' on the eastern bank. "More and more of them comin', Tim Piper. Ain't to cut teeth they bring them long rifles."

I nodded grimly.

For days thereafter my dreams were filled with nightmare scenes. I saw long lines of Mexicans tearin' through a confused rabble of Texas riflemen, stabbin' right and left. I saw Zach pleadin' for mercy while a bayonet pierced his heart. It wasn't long before I lay there, too, shiverin' with fear as the soldiers set the ferry afire and slew J. C. and Ruth Alice, then Jupe and the boys. Me they always saved for last.

"El Presidente has only one answer for rebels!" a young-lookin' officer cried. Then the bayonet touched my chest, and I awoke in a cold sweat.

"You shouldn't worry yourself needlessly," Ruth Alice scolded me when Leander and Titus told her of my miseries.

"Figure there's no need?" I asked her. Her fretful eyes answered me.

December brought the sharp claws of winter to the land. I was off choppin' stove wood bare-chested one afternoon, and by dusk the sky turned black, and the wind whipped up as bad an ice storm as I ever saw. Every inch of the public house was coated with sheets of ice, and J. C. had to use an ax to open the door come mornin'. The well froze solid, and the stock up at the corrals was half dead of cold. Half a foot of snow covered the ground, and trees were split in two by the weight of their ice-coated branches.

As for the ferry, it was painted white with ice and frozen in the shallows. Jupe did his best to free it by choppin' at the ice hunks, but the work only exhausted him. The ferry was trapped.

I was glad. The notion of pullin' it across the river with

that north wind cuttin' through everythin' movin' didn't pleasure me a particle. And we had no ferry customers anyway. Wasn't even a javelina movin'!

"So much for Burleson's army," J. C. said as we huddled around the table with our three boarders. "Won't be many of those soldiers stay through this sort of storm."

I hoped that was so, for I was missin' Zach. I hadn't had a letter from New Orleans lately and I was in sore need of a friendly word. Leander and Titus finally goaded me into wrestlin' with 'em, and I sharpened some sticks so we three could go after javelinas if the weather improved. Still, it wasn't the same.

As Christmas neared, we began to get some news out of Bexar. In late November Burleson and his little army had caught some Mexican foragers out in the open and cut 'em down. There'd been some shootin' in the town itself, but General Cos kept his army holed up in ole Mission Concepción and at the Alamo, another ole mission at the edge of town that served as a kind of fort now. Cos had plenty of cannons and lots of powder, and with winter comin' on, it didn't seem likely he was in danger. I guess that's why when a band of men passed through Washington claimin' Cos had surrendered his whole army—eleven hundred soldiers—we didn't much believe it.

"Sure he did," Noah Byars said. "And I shot the moon out of the sky last night, too."

Then Zach returned, tellin' the same tale, and J. C. dragged him into the public house and pleaded for the whole story. Titus and Leander were hoppin' 'round screamin', and the boarders begged for news, too.

"Well," Zach began as he started peelin' off layers of hides and blankets, "winter hit us hard. There were those spoke for endin' the campaign then and there, goin' home where we could find food and a warm fire. Some did leave. Then Ben Milam, a real old-time Texican with a taste for corn liquor and hard fightin', gave a shout. 'Who'll go with ole Ben Milam into Bexar?' he yelled. First one company and then another joined him. Folks were cold and tired, but pretty soon the shoutin' brought our blood to a boil, and we were hot to tackle the Mexicans.

" 'Why should they be sleepin' in warm beds and eatin' their fill when this is our country?' Cap'n Hanks asked. We all of us grumbled about it, and we were sure ready to fight Cos or Santa Anna or the devil himself if it came down to it. We marched to town, and just short of daybreak on December 5, we broke the Mexican pickets. Soon there were Texicans all over the place. We went down one street, and another company took the next. The Mexican soldiers never got themselves formed up, and soon they were runnin' for their lives 'cause our shootin' was right on the mark. Their guns lacked the range, and they weren't used to fixin' their target and hittin' him with one shot like a man out here who's always shy of powder."

"Go on," I pleaded.

"First big fight was in Concepción Square. Ben Milam was still leadin' us, and I think it was there he got shot stone cold dead. That was on the third day, I think. Wasn't a one of us to be held back now, not with ole Ben dead and the memory of his words ringin' in our ears. We chased Cos into the Alamo, but a fair bit of his army was already shot or captured. Short of food and facin' a mob of bloodthirsty devils, he finally asked for terms. December 10 he gave it up, and we took over Bexar."

"And Cos?" J. C. asked.

"We took their cannons and muskets and sent 'em

back to Mexico proper with a parole not to fight us again," Zach explained. "We've got garrisons in Bexar and Goliad. The rest of us went home for winter."

"Santa Anna will be in Texas come spring," J. C. said, shakin' his head sadly. "And we'll wish we hadn't sent Cos's army back to fight us again."

"He signed a parole," Zach objected.

"To a bunch of rebels?" J. C. cried. "Figure El Presidente will put much stock in that? He slaughters rebels, remember? Even when they surrender to him on terms."

I frowned, and even Zach lost a little of his bluster. But afterward he cheered up when I found him some hot cider and Ruth Alice cooked him a bowl of stew.

"I didn't come back empty-handed, you know," Zach whispered when he finished. He led me outside. Back of the woodpile he'd left a cowhide bag. Inside were all manner of things—a Mexican soldier's tall hat pierced by a rifle ball, a bayonet, an officer's pistol, and a good powder horn he handed to me.

"What for?" I asked. "I don't have a rifle."

"Yeah, you do," he said, leadin' me to where a pair of fine Kentucky rifles lay protected by oilskins. "Belonged to Joshua Denby, who was cut down the first mornin', Tim. He told me to take 'em and see they got used to defend Texas liberty."

"But . . ."

"I put 'em to good use in Bexar, Tim. Only need one, though."

"I don't understand," I said, noticin' the grave look that came over his face.

"I thought to save it for your birthday," he told me. "But I see Ruth Alice hasn't got much use for soldiers, and she'd have my hide for givin' it to you. Besides, if J. C.'s right, you'll need it 'fore then."

"Zach?"

"Just remember what I said. It's for defendin' Texas liberty. When the time's right, you'll know what to do with her. I know you that well."

"You figure I'm fit to march with you against Santa Anna?" I asked.

"Not then," he said, restin' a hand on my shoulder and lookin' at me with solemn eyes. "Lord, I pray not at all. But if it comes to it, I know you'll be one to stand to the cause. Nobody ever treed by a javelina skedaddled from a mere Napoleon."

NINE

CHRISTMAS CAME AND WENT, with me sharin' as much of the celebratin' as I could manage. It was the first Christmas I'd been away from Mama and my brothers and sister, and all the months on the Brazos didn't soften the hurt bein' far away brought. Still, I had a good letter the week before, with even a note from Michael in it, and Mama'd sent warm mittens and a woolen scarf.

They were needed. Those first months of 1836 were as bitter cold as any I could remember. When ice and snow weren't fallin', the wind was howlin' and sendin' freezin' slivers through my ribs. Even bundled in one of J. C.'s old woolen sweaters 'neath my buckskin jacket, I shook myself half to death from the chill.

Nights were hardest. January and February were slack seasons for innkeepers, Ruth Alice told me, but with more and more folks comin' down the La Bahía Road toward Washington or San Felipe, the three rent-out rooms were always full, and I climbed the ladder into the fireless loft each evenin'. When the cold's bite was at its worst, Leander, Titus, and I all heaped our quilts and blankets atop my bed and crawled underneath together. It was a little like passin' the night 'tween a pair of river eels, what with their squirmin' 'round, but bein' huddled up like that chased off some of the melancholy I'd felt since Christmas.

We had a fair degree of excitement in town. All sorts of famous people crossed the river and paid calls on Washington. In January the bear killer himself, Davy Crockett of Tennessee, passed the night with us. I'd grown up hearin' stories of Davy, how he'd fought the Creeks and wrestled bears. He'd been a congressman, too, but he told us the people had gone and "unelected" him. He was a yarn spinner to equal Captain Tom. Once word got 'round he was in Washington, people gathered to say their howdies. Zach, hearin' he was at our place, came over and passed the night in the loft in order to listen to the evenin' conversation.

"He's shorter'n I figured," Zach told me later. "And where's his buckskins?"

"Wool's warmer in winter," I answered. "Bet he's got a skin cap packed away in his saddlebags."

We were both impressed by the beautiful long rifle he carried, though. Bess, Crockett called the gun, and its stock was oiled and polished shinier'n Ruth Alice's walnut table!

"I'm bound for Bexar," Crockett declared as he bid us farewell. "Hear there's excitement brewin' there. And cheap land to be had," he added.

In truth, there was somethin' brewin', but I would've called it plain, old-fashioned trouble. Santa Anna, who was comin' more and more to be thought a dictator both in Texas and Mexico, had acted pretty much as J. C. had supposed. Rumors were flyin' 'bout how El Presidente was in Saltillo with six thousand troops. He'd already rearmed Cos, and there were other soldiers comin', too.

"We're all of us in peril!" Mr. Lott exclaimed. "Thousands of Mexican soldiers are marchin' north, and we don't even have a government!"

Other people said pretty much the same. One, a tall fellow named Sam Houston who'd once been governor of Tennessee, grumbled how we Texicans were our own worst enemies. We had armies all over the place and nobody in charge.

Zach agreed. "Never knew an army with so many colonels!" he complained. "I hear there's a company downriver where they've got three colonels, twelve captains, six sergeants, and only one private."

It didn't make for too good an army, not when nobody'd take orders, and everyone set off for one place or another without tellin' anybody else. I guess that's why the people, bein' fed up, called another convention, this one at Washington. In no time every spare bed for miles 'round was full! We had delegates sharin' the loft and others housed in the warehouses toward town. On top of that, soldiers from the United States, spurred by Stephen Austin's pleas published in the newspapers, started showin' up at the ferry.

The convention was called for March 1, but by the last week of February we already had one whole company of Kentuckians camped on the river, and more'n a few others scattered here and there north and south of town. By then there was news from Bexar.

"The Mexican army's come," Zach called to me as Jupe and I were pullin' a band of newcomers up to the west bank. "They're in Bexar! Buck Travis's sent word."

Zach meant the news for me, but the ferry passengers heard, too, and they embarked on a lively chorus of boastin'. They didn't think much of Santa Anna or Mexicans in general, and were sure a small band of Texicans, with the help of their American neighbors, could sweep the invaders right back across the Rio Bravo.

"We'll go down to Bexar and do it ourselves, won't we, boys?" a burly Georgian cried. "Give us a few squirrel guns, and we'll settle this fight quick enough."

"Will you?" J. C. asked, meetin' the ferry as it touched shore. "Takes more'n a mouth to fight a war. And to win one, well, you need the rest of your head workin'."

The newcomers made a rush at J. C., but he produced a pistol from his belt, and they backed off fast enough.

"Can you see 'em chargin' Mexican bayonets?" Zach asked, and the soldiers camped along the river hooted. Wasn't anytime 'fore the Georgians were known as Taylor's Talkers, after their burly leader. In their defense, though, they didn't waste any time headin' on down the La Bahía Road to join up with Colonel James Fannin at Goliad.

Once my ferryin' duties were finished for the day, I headed into town with Zach to read Buck Travis's dispatch from Bexar. It seemed odd how popular Travis had grown to be. Half the folks in Washington were willin' to hang that Alabama lawyer a few months back. Now he was a colonel in the Texican army, in command of the Alamo since Big Jim Bowie had taken sick. Davy Crockett was there, too, along with a hundred or so others. I knew a few of 'em from the ferry, and I wondered how their families took them bein' in Bexar with the Mexicans closin' in.

The dispatch was nailed to the door of the long, unfinished hall across from Mr. Byars's smithy. Zach and I worked our way through a small crowd until we could see the words clearly. They tore at my heart, and I'll never forget 'em.

Commandancy of the Alamo
Bexar, Feby 24th, 1836

To the People of Texas and All Americans in
the World—

Fellow citizens and compatriots:

I am besieged by a thousand or more of the Mexicans
under Santa Anna. I have sustained continual
bombardment & cannonade for 24 hours & have not
lost a man. The enemy had demanded a surrender at
discretion, otherwise, the garrison are to be put to the
sword, if the fort is taken. I have answered the demand
with a cannon shot, & our flag still waves proudly from
the walls. *I shall never surrender or retreat.* Then I call on
you in the name of Liberty, of patriotism and
everything dear to the American character, to come to
our aid, with all dispatch. The enemy is receiving
reinforcements daily & will no doubt increase to three
or four thousand in four or five days. If this call is
neglected, I am determined to sustain myself as long as
possible & die like a soldier who never forgets what is
due to his own honor & that of his country.

   VICTORY OR DEATH.

William Barrett Travis
Lt. Co. Comdt.

   P.S. the Lord is on our side—When the enemy
appeared in sight we had three bushels of corn. We
have since found in deserted houses 80 or 90 bushels
and got into the walls 20 or 30 head of Beeves.

   "Well, I never knew ole Buck had a big long name like
that," one of the men remarked.

"Looks like Santy Anny's in trouble now," another added.

Zach gazed at me sourly, though, and we left the others jokin' away in the road or hurryin' over to Lott's tavern to have a whiskey.

"I'm goin'," Zach told me. "Been thinkin' on it, and now I'm sure. I got my horse saddled in the trees. Be sayin' my good-byes to my family and headin' for Bexar. If the worst happens, you'll look in on my brothers, won't you?"

"Zach?" I asked. "There's a hundred men down at the river can go. It's not for you . . ."

"Travis wasn't only writin' to them," Zach said. "Those words were for me, too."

"Wait up," I called as he surged ahead. "I got a blanket I can let you have. You're sure to need it tonight."

"I will," he said, slowin'. "Tim, you remember what I said when I gave you that rifle?"

"Sure, Zach."

"You give some time to practicin' 'cause you may come to have use for it. Understand?"

I nodded. When we got to the public house, I slipped past a circle of newcomers and made my way inside. The common room was crowded, but nobody paid me much mind as I climbed the ladder and took a blanket from on top of the pile of straw where I'd been sleepin' of late. I went back downstairs and gave Zach the blanket. He gripped my hand firmly, like Papa did when he made a bargain back in Natchez. I hadn't altogether noticed it happenin', but Zach Merkins looked like a full-grown man.

"Don't you go get shot now," I said as I tried to steady myself and hold back the urge to get sentimental.

"Do my best to stay free of holes," he answered. I

watched him walk down the hill and fetch his horse. Then he mounted up and headed toward Bexar.

Zach Merkins was Washington's answer to Buck Travis.

By the time the delegates to the convention met March 1, there were other letters from Travis. These weren't tacked to the door or read aloud, but we got hints of what was in 'em. Colonel Fannin down in Goliad had been sent for, but he wasn't comin'. There were soldiers here, there, everywhere, but they weren't bound for Bexar, either. Some of the delegates proposed leavin' the convention and ridin' as a group to rescue Travis, but Sam Houston, who got himself appointed general of the whole army, said it was best the government organize itself, else there'd be more Alamos. After all, who was it got Buck Travis holed up with three bushels of corn?

"It won't be a short war," Mr. Lott announced when he and J. C. turned over their warehouses and corrals to use as a military commissary. "Armies need food in their bellies and clothes on their backs."

While some of the other town boys got to gaze through the open door and windows at the convention, I was busy down at the ferry. It grated at me some, hearin' the convention was busy declarin' Texas independent and writin' a constitution. I wanted to be there, see it happenin'. But while others got to have a look, I did ferry most of the important folks across.

They were a mixed lot, the delegates. Some, like Lorenzo de Zavala, were Mexicans of good families and high education. Señor de Zavala had held office in the Mexican government before havin' a fallin'-out with Santa Anna. General Cos had offered a reward for his head, but he was a man who loved freedom. I took note of his good manners and fine clothes, and he left me a silver peso and a word of encouragement when he stepped off the ferry.

Tom Rusk was a youngish fellow with red hair who had folks comparin' him to Tom Jefferson. He wound up Secretary of War, a job that seemed sure to tax his energies. He, like Sam Houston, was a talker, and he was especially prone to urge what men hadn't already joined the army to do so.

Mr. Robert Potter, who was given charge of the navy I didn't know Texas had, was only a hair older'n Rusk. He was from the Carolinas, and it showed in his speech. He'd served in the Carolina legislature and the U.S. Navy, but what drew a smile to my face was that he knew Captain Tom and had heard him talk of me.

There were a fair number of wealthy men there, and several who'd served in the U.S. Congress. The task of writin' a Declaration of Independence fell to a Tennesseean name of George Childress.

"'Course he had a fair example to follow," Mr. Byars said, meanin' the one the American colonies had come up with. Me, I never read that other one, and I judged gettin' anythin' written with so much goin' on to be a considerable accomplishment.

The delegates weren't all rich men, though. Many were the same brand of buckskin-dressed farmers and adventurers that boarded so often at J. C.'s public house. Most didn't go anywhere without a brace of pistols or at least a bowie knife, and they near drank the town dry durin' their stay. In fact, Jupe and I brought in soldiers, food, and arms, but the thing that interested our visitors most were the jugs of corn liquor and bottles of wine bound for Lott's tavern.

All in all, they did their job fast and well. The Declaration of Independence was made March 2, and a wild bit of shoutin' and drinkin' followed that. The soldiers shot off their muskets and hollered taunts at the Mexicans, who were out of hearin'.

"I thank you all for throwin' this fine shebang on my birthday," Sam Houston told 'em. Two days later he took charge of the army and dragged what there was of it camped along the Brazos with him to Gonzales.

"It's about time someone thought of that," Ruth Alice cried. She was fond of Zach, and though she never said it, I knew she was worryin' after him as much as I was. There'd been less news from Bexar lately, and all of the news we had gotten had been bad. One message did get through concernin' Buck Travis's little boy Charlie, who was stayin' in town with the Ayres family.

"Take care of my little boy," I heard it read. "If I perish, he will have nothing but the proud recollection that he is the son of a man who died for his country."

I didn't care for the sound of those words, knowin' Travis wouldn't die alone. With him was the best friend I'd ever had.

News from Bexar stopped altogether after that, but the rumors didn't. One had General Houston and Colonel Fannin surprisin' Santa Anna in his sleep and capturin' the whole blamed Mexican army in their nightshirts. Another said Travis had fought back a dozen assaults and was bleedin' the Mexicans white. Two families who'd piled their belongin's in a wagon and fled from Gonzales carried the darkest version. Santa Anna had holed the Alamo's walls and killed the gallant garrison down to the last man and boy.

That night I couldn't sleep. Winter wouldn't let go its hold on the land, and I shivered with cold as I lay beside Titus and Leander in the straw. Outside a wolf was howlin' eerily, and the clouds had swallowed the moon, robbin' us of the faint trace of light that seeped through the gaps between the oak planks of the walls.

"Hear that?" Titus whispered. "Somethin's gone and died."

"Naw, it's just a wolf," Leander insisted.

"Remember Mama's story 'bout the wolves mournin' their friends?" Titus asked. "Ole Ezra Jenkins was pretty sick."

"Ezra Jenkins hated wolves," Leander argued. "Now get to sleep. You're keepin' us all awake."

There was a murmur of agreement from the beds on the far side of the loft, and Titus hushed. The wolf went on howlin', though, and Titus burrowed his way under my arm and shook till I steadied him with my hand.

"It's just a story," he whispered. "But sometimes stories are true."

Yes, I thought. Sometimes.

The next mornin', March 15, the day they say Caesar was stabbed all those years back in Rome, news came for certain that the Alamo'd fallen.

"And the men?" I asked. "I had a friend there."

"We all lost friends," the dispatch rider declared. "But they'll be remembered . . . and avenged."

I didn't care, though. All I knew was I'd lost Zach.

"Can I borrow a horse?" I asked J. C. "Somebody ought to go and tell Zach's mama."

"John Lott's already sent a boy," J. C. told me. "I'm sorry about Zach. I liked him. He did what he felt was his duty."

"I know," I said, swallowin' the tears that wanted to flow. "But that doesn't make him any less dead."

TEN

THE FALL OF THE ALAMO, and Bexar with it, spread a flood of despair over Washington. The delegates made speeches praisin' the devotion of the slain martyrs or accusin' their companions of neglectin' Buck Travis's pleas for aid. Some blamed Fannin, who had set out for Bexar only to turn back because a wagon broke down.

"He'll have his own worries soon enough," J. C. warned. "As will Sam Houston. Santa Anna'll have his eyes on them . . . and then us."

I didn't reply. I felt like I'd come home from a funeral, and I had no heart to talk . . . or work . . . or even cry. I was numb. The world was colder'n the north wind, and all I managed to do was wander around the ferry landin' and remember Zach.

Later I took the rifle down to Noah Byars and had him give it a look over.

"It's a fine rifle, Tim," he declared. "But it's not been cleaned in a time. Let me show you how to do it. After the Alamo, most Texas boys'll have need of such knowledge. Be needin' the men for the army."

"Not J. C.," I told him. "He and John Lott are runnin' the commissary."

"Well, that's true," he confessed. "Still, you're nearin'

fifteen. Boys that young served and died with Travis, you know."

I did know. All too well.

It was while cleanin' the rifle I decided to join the army. Zach had seen it comin', this day when I'd have to shoulder a gun and take my place with the men. I had whiskers on my chin, after all, and I was near four inches over five feet tall. Some men were no bigger, after all!

I didn't tell J. C. right away. Instead I went down into the bottoms and put the rifle to use. I'd learned to shoot when I was just eight, and I knew how to ram down a ball and splash powder in the pan, remembered not to use too much waddin', and checked my flint. I lifted the heavy gun in my arms and made sure the barrel was level. Then, boom! I shot limbs off a live oak and blew rocks off a fallen log. Later on I hid along a javelina trail and shot a wild pig for the supper pot.

When I brought the javelina to Ruth Alice, she stared at the rifle in my arms and frowned. It hadn't been easy keepin' that gun hidden since December, but I thought I'd managed to do it. Somethin' in her eyes told me she knew all along, and I thought maybe Zach had broken down and told.

"So you've taken to hunting, have you?" she asked.

"Was mainly practicin' my aim," I explained. "Zach suggested it."

"Zach's dead," she said sadly.

"Yeah. But he gave me the rifle 'fore he left, and he said if the Alamo was to fall, maybe I'd have my chance to fight for Texas."

"He had no right to say such a thing!" she argued. "You're just a boy, hardly taller than Leander. This is a man's fight. It's not like hunting, Timmy. My brother was killed fighting the British in Canada. People make up tales about heroes, but war isn't like that at all. It's mean, and it's dirty, and people die, especially if they're young and thin and not used to rough life."

"I've known hardship," I told her. "How many folks ever have to leave their family and go to another country?"

"We're family, too, you know."

"Sure, I do. That's part of the reason I have to go. J. C. has his job. He can't go to the army. I can."

"You'll be killed like Zach!"

"Maybe. But I got to go just the same," I told her.

J. C. came in then, and he took Ruth Alice's side right away. "You're doin' your part at the ferry," he pointed out.

"You don't either of you understand," I complained. "Seems all I do's stand 'round and watch things happen. Years from now folks'll tell how they watched the signin' of the Declaration of Independence that set Texas off from Mexico, and I'll say I was ferryin' corn liquor 'cross the Brazos at the time. They wrote some fine words on that paper, J. C., but they don't mean a thing if Santa Anna marches through here and puts a torch to it all. Zach left me this rifle knowin' my turn'd come. Don't you figure it has?"

"I promised your mama I'd look after you," J. C. hollered. "Tim, you've the makin' of a good man. I couldn't stop Zach. I'm not his father. But 'round here, I'm the closest thing to one you got."

"Maybe so," I admitted. "I know I'm not much to look at, just bones with a little skin stretched on top, but the ferry's made me strong. I can march all day and not tire. If food's scarce, I can make snares, and I hit what I shoot at. I know you'll worry, and I confess it'll be hard leavin'. The day I left New Orleans I set off on a man's trail, though, and it's too late to go back and try to be a boy. Señor de Zavala told me Texas would need good men like me. Well, I got to give it a try."

"You'd be making a mistake," Ruth Alice said, restin' her hands on my shoulders.

"Wouldn't be the first time, would it, J. C.?" I asked, managin' the best smile I could.

They looked at each other a minute, and I knew then that they wouldn't stop me. I gave Ruth Alice a hug, and I shook J. C.'s hand. That night I told Leander and Titus. I prayed the wolf wouldn't howl.

Next mornin', March 16, the delegates in Washington approved a constitution. And I signed the muster book and became a private soldier in the Army of Texas.

ELEVEN

EıGHT of us were sworn into service that day, and we were assigned to a small company of Kentuckians commanded by Captain Josiah Fitch, late of Louisville. Captain Fitch, to hear him tell it, knew more 'bout soldierin' than Sam Houston or Tom Rusk or even George Washington. He'd fought at Horseshoe Bend, he claimed, and been a bigger hero'n Sam Houston.

"Houston was a lieutenant," the captain explained. "I was a corporal barely older'n you youngsters."

Knowin' how likely it was for me to prove a hero, I quickly figured Joe Fitch to have no particular acquaintance with the truth.

Before headin' south to fight the Mexicans, Fitch turned us over to a quartermaster sergeant, who in turn took us to J. C. and John Lott. They looked us over, gave us each a blanket, made sure we had a water flask, and issued us shot and powder.

I was straddlin' a log, hollowin' out a two-necked Mexican gourd to use for a water flask, when a pair of powerful hands lifted me into the air and turned me head over heels.

"Was you goin' to go and sneak off to the army and never tell me a word of it!" Jupiter hollered.

"I would've said good-bye," I told him as I managed to

regain my feet. "Only I'm no good at it, and I figured you'd be mad for me leavin' you all the work."

"Madder if you'd gone off unprotected," he said, handin' me a small charm made of a chicken's wishbone, some ribbon, and a copper penny. "This here's a mad stone," he added, puttin' a small stone in my pocket. "Know how to use it?"

I shook my head, and he scowled.

"Thought you an educated man, too," Jupe grumbled. "You worry over it. Say you got an ache. Rub it wid this stone and put the ache in the rock."

"Does it work?" I asked.

"Do for me," he said, smilin'. "Don't know it'd take a bayonet out of your belly, but it chases fever."

"Thanks, Jupe," I said, noddin' a kind of unspoken partin'. "I'll miss you."

"Miss you, too, Tim Piper. Every time I got to pull that ferry 'cross the river all by myself."

I laughed, then returned to my labors. After we all had gourds, we filled 'em from J. C.'s well and got into a line of sorts. Each mess was given a corn grinder and a coffeepot, and I wound up carryin' the pot, havin' no extra clothes to lug in my blanket roll. Captain Fitch grouped the youngest together for eatin', and for marchin' as well, so when we finally headed out I tramped along beside a boy from upriver named Billy Stewart. Billy was just turnin' thirteen, but claimed to be older. Just ahead of us Jonah Brent and Noah Hayes, whose papas farmed along the west bank of the Brazos, rounded out our mess. Jonah was sixteen, and Noah was a year younger. When the captain was up ahead, barkin' orders at the older fellows, we talked some.

"Where'd you come by that rifle?" Noah asked. "I never knew you to have a gun."

"Not much chance to use one, workin' the ferry," I told him. "Zach Merkins brought it to me from Bexar in December. It belonged to a man got killed fightin' Cos."

"Zach was at the Alamo," Jonah said sadly. "I went huntin' with him some when we was younger."

"Santa Anna's got a lot to answer for," I said, coughin' from the dust raised by the men ahead of us.

"Guess we'll be bringin' him to heel," Noah declared.

We were four days marchin' on parched corn and boiled beef before we joined General Houston and the rest of the army on the Colorado River. It was close to sixty miles on that dusty road, but only half as far as we'd expected. For while we were hurryin' toward General Houston, he'd been hurryin' toward us.

"This Houston fellow's goin' backwards," Jonah pointed out when we made camp. "Seems like he's in a powerful rush to run away."

"You boys ain't seen nothin'," a soldier from a nearby company called. "We went and burned Gonzales before leavin' the Guadalupe. Half the country's packed up and skedaddled. They call it the Runaway Scrape! Scrape together what you can and run—away!"

A little later we saw it for ourselves. Long lines of ox carts and wagons full of furniture, pots, steamer trunks, and little children hurried eastward. Sometimes the people cursed us for runnin' away, and boys tossed rocks in our direction.

"Cowards!" one woman cried. "My man died with Travis! You call yourselves an army. Fight!"

We were willin' enough, but General Houston was mighty shy 'bout puttin' us to the test. On March 21, the Mexican General Sesma arrived on the far bank of the river with Santa Anna's vanguard. They were camped only a couple of miles upstream, and we set to cleanin' our rifles and readyin' ourselves for a battle. General Houston stomped around the camp like he was ready, too, and he sent the scouts out to find us a place to ford the river. Four days passed, though, and except for practicin' our aim some by shootin' at ducks or overcurious Mexican scouts, all we did was sit around and get hungry.

"Word is the general's waitin' for Fannin to come up from Victoria," Noah told us at dinner. "Then we'll fall on Sesma from north and south."

But when the scouts finally spotted a column movin' toward us, it wasn't Fannin.

"Mexican cavalry comin'," the word spread through camp. What was worse, General Gaona with close to a thousand men was crossin' the Colorado upstream at Bastrop. Looked like if anybody got trapped it would be us!

General Houston didn't give the Mexicans the chance, though. Early on the 26th, the day 'fore Palm Sunday, we formed up into companies and set off north and east— toward the Brazos.

All along the way everyone was wonderin' the same thing. What had become of Fannin? He had close to eight hundred men, it was said. Among 'em was Billy Stewart's papa.

"I should've gone with him," Billy grumbled. "Colonel Fannin went to West Point, you know. He's likely up ahead fightin' like we should be! Papa's a captain, you know, and a better man'n Joe Fitch, by gosh!"

When we did learn of Fannin, we were sorry for it. Around noon the day after leavin' the Colorado, a pair of nigh frantic and half-naked men stumbled up to our column.

"Lord be praised!" one cried. "We're saved."

"Salvation!" the other screamed.

Billy broke ranks and rushed toward 'em. Others did the same. When I caught up with Billy, he explained breathlessly how one of those fellows was in his papa's company.

"They're from Fannin's army!" the cry went up.

Indeed they were. In fact, by their account they were about all that was left. West Point trained or not, James Fannin had done poorly. First, he let a pair of adventurers split off small bands and get themselves killed at San Patricio, huntin' mustangs. Then a small column was run down by cavalry at Refugio. With the Mexicans hot on his heels, Fannin abandoned the old Mexican fort at Goliad and set off for Victoria. He made camp in the open, with no cover or water, and the Mexican cavalry under General Urrea fell on 'em. Surrounded, runnin' short of food, water, and powder, and bombarded by two Mexican cannons, Fannin did what Buck Travis swore *he* wouldn't—surrendered.

The bitter news was yet to come, though. Fannin thought to save his men, but Santa Anna ordered the whole lot of 'em taken out and shot. So early on Palm Sunday the army paraded past the Presidio La Bahía in Goliad, and the Mexican guards opened fire.

"Like shootin' blindfolded chickens," one of the survivors told us. "I saw 'em take wounded men and throw 'em down on the ground, then bayonet 'em. There was a boy no older'n twelve beside me, come to blow the fife while we marched. They shot him three, four times, and he lay there bleedin' and prayin' for mercy. He got none."

"How'd you get away?" Billy asked.

"Hid under the dead," the first one explained. "Then made a run for it. Were seven or eight of us in the beginnin', but the Mexican cavalry run down the rest."

"And the officers?" Billy cried. "Maybe they were spared?"

"No, they're dead," the fugitive answered. "Shot inside the fort. Even Colonel Fannin, curse his hide. If he'd let us fight on, at least we'd have taken a few of those devils with us."

We managed to find a few scraps of clothes for the men, but only one accepted our invite to join the army.

"I got a wife and three kids somewhere," the other explained. "We came to Texas in hopes of gettin' good land cheap. All we've found is death and hardship. I'm goin' back to Georgia."

I thought perhaps the officers might force the man to stay, his bein' sworn into service and all, but no attempt was made to keep him from leavin'. Moreover, when we got to San Felipe on the 28th, close to three hundred others demanded furloughs and set off to tend their families.

"We'll be back once our wives are seen to," some promised.

"I got to see my boy's gettin' a crop in," another said.

Many made no promises, and I doubted we'd see half of 'em in the army again. We hadn't fired a shot, and already the army was meltin' away.

Billy Stewart left us, too.

"Papa's dead," he told Captain Fitch. "I got to tell Mama, help her move the little ones to safety."

"Your duty's here, son," Fitch argued.

"I know my duty, and I ain't your son or nobody else's!" Billy shouted. "I'll be back to fight that Santa Anna if I'm the only one in Texas to do it. Some things cry for vengeance! Blood will have blood!"

I was pretty dissatisfied with army life in general, and with the general in particular! Just upriver lay Washington. My family and ole Jupe were there. Or maybe they'd already taken off for the Sabine River and the safety of Louisiana. I thought about Zach's family, about Travis's boy Charlie stayin' at the Ayres house. And I imagined the government of Texas runnin', too, with its bold Declaration comin' to nothin'.

"Is this what you died for, Zach?" I whispered as I walked guard duty along the river. "All those men with Travis, and these others shot down at Goliad!"

I remembered Davy Crockett entertainin' us in the common room. I thought back to sittin' with Zach in that oak while a mad javelina circled below. And I wondered how many of the soldiers I ferried across the Brazos would live to see summer.

On March 29, General Houston issued marchin' orders again. Another retreat was in the works. This time, though, there was out and out rebellion. Mosely Baker's company crossed the Brazos and waited on the east bank, refusin' to budge. They set to erectin' earthworks and swore they'd defend the crossin' against the whole of Mexico if it came to it.

Wily Martin took his company downriver to Fort Bend. He burned the town and crossed to the east bank, sayin' the Mexicans weren't gettin' past him, either.

"We'll fight even if the rest of the army crosses the Sabine!" one soldier shouted.

"The Sabine?" another howled. "Skedaddle Sam won't stop till he sees the magnolias bloomin' on the far side of the Mississip."

Captain Fitch kept what was left of his little company with the general. We were down to twenty-two, the rest either headin' off to look after family or takin' ill. We were all of us hungry, for the country'd been given to cotton, and we were hard-pressed to find a stray cow or even a chicken. Parched corn was now a treat, and coffee was bringin' in a silver dollar a cup.

Late that afternoon we reached a small creek. As we began crossin' over, rain came down in torrents. Amid the mud and the cold, some men just sat down and wept. Others went a little mad and threw off their clothes, dancin' naked and singin' like loons.

"Figure this is the finish of us?" Noah whispered as we splashed our way through the creek.

"Don't seem like much of an army," I confessed as I watched the mob struggle north beside the Brazos.

"Oh, we're an army, all right," Jonah declared. "Army of fools. We been marchin' half a month, and we're nigh back where we started. We've fought no battles nor hardly seen a Mexican, but we've lost a third of our strength, and Fannin's men, too. The Texas Republic didn't last long, did it?"

We were so discouraged and wet and tired that we hardly noticed the tall man on horseback who suddenly made his way among us.

"Bring the men to a halt, gentlemen!" a voice bellowed. "I'll have a word with 'em."

Officers shouted commands, and one or two companies formed. Ours stumbled along as before, ignorin' Captain Fitch's curses. It was the wild movements of the horseman that brought us to a stop. We half suspected he'd trample us otherwise.

"It's the general," Noah told me.

I didn't much care who it was, but he managed to hold me still as General Houston, wrapped in a soggy black dress coat and as wet as the rest of us, addressed his army.

"My friends," he began, "I am told that evilly disposed persons have told you I am going to march you to the

Redlands. This is fake. I'm going to lead you into the Brazos bottom near Groce's to a position where you can whip the enemy even if he comes ten to one, and where you can get an abundant supply of corn."

For once there was a muffled cheer, though I think it was more for the promise of the corn than in expectation of a successful fight. We were cold and hungry, and I wager we'd have fought the devil himself for the promise of some dry ground for a bed and a hot meal in our bellies.

And so we made our way to Groce's Plantation, one of the biggest places on the river. Mr. Groce had large stocks of everythin', and he offered 'em to General Houston.

"Better you men enjoy the fruits of my labor than El Presidente!" he was supposed to've said.

We erected our simple cloth tents, or what was left of them, in lines by company, and we enjoyed a rare visit by the steamer *Yellowstone*. The ship brought news of the government, now down south in Harrisburg, and it also brought us beef and coffee and a bit of sugar from J. C.'s warehouses upriver.

Here, too, a young hothead named Mirabeau Lamar first came to our attention. This Lamar suggested takin' three hundred men aboard *Yellowstone* and settin' off after Gaona's northern column. In no time others proposed sendin' men here or there, roundin' up cattle, or surprisin' Sesma.

"Can't they see it's what Fannin did?" Noah asked, shakin' from a fever he caught crossin' the creek. "They'll just make it easy for the Mexicans. We have to stay together."

I thought so myself, but I knew, too, we wouldn't win anything runnin' away. And General Sesma didn't seem willin' to come to Groce's. Noah's fever worsened, though, and Jonah and I soon had all we could do tendin' him. I tried boilin' water and givin' him a hot wash like Mama used to do, but the ground was cold and damp, as were our blankets and clothes. I gave Jupe's mad stone a try, too, but its powers were beyond me. Noah's cough worsened, and his cheeks grew hollow. Finally I accepted the loan of a horse and took him up to Washington.

My heart stirred within me as I approached the town. All along the way we passed deserted farms, Noah's among 'em. I didn't have the heart to tell him, and he didn't open his eyes but twice.

"Am I goin' to see Mama soon?" he asked.

"No, but there's no town for doctors like Washington," I told him. "Don't you worry. We'll get you well."

I passed Dr. Hoxey's house first, and he took charge of Noah in a moment. I paced outside while the doctor peeled Noah's wet clothes and sweated him in hot blankets. Dr. Hoxey dosed him some, too, and afterward, when the cough eased, and Noah opened his eyes, the doctor showed me inside.

"Had us worried," I told Noah as his breathin' grew gentler.

"I had to find some way to get myself a dry bed," he answered. "Where we be?"

"Washington," I replied. "Almost home."

"Seen my folks?"

"I only saw Dr. Hoxey. If you feel all right, I'll ride down and say howdy to J. C. and Ruth Alice. Maybe Leander can ride out and fetch your mama."

"Be good to see her," Noah said, grinnin'. His eyes closed, and he drifted off into a peaceful sleep.

"He'll be fine, Tim," Dr. Hoxey assured me. "But his

soldierin' days are finished for now. You ride along and see your family. And tell Jupe to pocket his mad stones and leave the doctorin' to me."

"J. C. still here?" I asked.

"Not everyone's got skedaddle fever, you know. A few of us've stayed."

"Thanks, Doc," I said, fumblin' in my pockets for somethin' to give him.

"Don't you go and get me mad, Tim Piper," he growled. "I was tendin' this boy's ills 'fore you knew the light of day. Get on with you. And when you boys've licked Santa Anna, stop by and tell me how you did it. That'll be pay enough."

"Yes, sir," I promised. "We'll do it, too, you know."

"Never allowed elsewise," he said.

My visit with J. C. and Ruth Alice was brief. Washington was knowin' its share of hard times, too, though the ferry was doin' good business. But most folks had no money, and J. C. didn't accept a penny from anybody who had menfolk with Travis or Fannin or servin' with General Houston.

"Doesn't leave much of anybody," J. C. confessed, "but we're lucky. They've burned San Felipe, you know. Gonzales, too. Can't leave anything for El Presidente to use. If the Mexicans get close to Washington, the quartermasters have orders to fire the warehouses and sink the ferry. So I guess you'd better beat ole Santa Anna soon, Tim."

Jupe did a bit of poundin' on my back, and Ruth Alice gave my clothes a thorough scrub and insisted I do the same on myself. I passed the night in the loft with Titus and Leander hurlin' questions at me I couldn't answer.

"I don't know 'bout battles," I finally told 'em. "All we do is march."

I returned to Groce's two days later with the news that Noah was too sick to serve. Two other men were down with measles, and a quarter of the army had one thing or another. Chicken pox was said to have laid up half of Ned Burleson's regiment. That put Colonel Sidney Sherman to prancin' 'round claimin' his bunch of Kentuckians were better men. Then the pox hit them, too, and ole Ned had his revenge.

Those men who weren't sick took advantage of those peaceful April days to drill and practice their marksmanship. We learned to fight together, and for the first time we seemed to be an army. I caught General Houston noddin' his head and even smilin' when he thought we weren't lookin'. He seemed satisfied, and on April 12 we started crossin' over to the east bank of the Brazos.

"Runnin' again?" Jonah cried.

"Maybe," I muttered. "But it could be we're goin' to fight."

TWELVE

WHILE AT GROCE'S we'd taken on supplies and received new flints and fresh powder. More valuable was the gift from the people of Cincinnati—a pair of brass cannons dubbed the Twin Sisters. For a time we felt like an army again. We had artillery. But that feelin' passed.

What remained of our dwindlin' army stumbled eastward. The weather was nasty, and a continual rain made me envious of Noah, who was no doubt restin' easy back in Washington while we trudged along in the mud. We were all of us grumblin', and the wretched collection of folks streamin' out behind us didn't raise anybody's spirits.

"Look at 'em," Jonah told me as he pushed his soggy mop of blond hair back from his forehead. "They're beaten. It's on their faces."

"And us?" I asked.

"Yeah, us, too," he confessed. "Looks like all Texas is headed for the Sabine."

I wasn't so sure. General Houston had told us he wasn't goin' to the Redlands, that stretch of sandy pine forest along the Louisiana border. I remembered how tall and proud he'd been when the convention delegates gave him the army. A man like that didn't just up and run away. Leastwise I hoped not. If we did there'd be nobody 'tween Santa Anna and Washington.

That night as Jonah and I lay in our little tent that was now half empty, I wondered what sort of mischance had led us to such a state. When I closed my eyes, I was set upon by new nightmares. Mexican soldiers lined the La Bahía Road while J. C. led my friends in a column of twos. Muskets barked, and bullets tore through Ruth Alice's chest, struck down J. C. and ole Jupe, killed Noah Byars and John Lott. In the end only Leander and Titus were left, and the Mexicans chased after 'em with bayonets.

"Timmy, help us!" they called.

"I give you that rifle," a phantom Zach chided. "Use it!"

But I was marchin' 'cross the Sabine with Sam Houston, leavin' Texas to the ravages of the Mexican army.

I awoke boilin' mad and ready to bite into somebody. Jonah saw it straight away and kept clear. Captain Fitch came round to order us to form, and I looked at him hatefully.

"Marchin' again?" I asked. "Bet it pleases you to see us gettin' close to your home. Mine's upriver in Washington!"

"Wrong, Piper!" he scolded. "Your home's this army. Now get to your feet and fold up this pitiful excuse for a tent. We've got soldierin' to do."

"Soldierin'?" Jonah cried.

"We're off to whip the Mexicans!" Fitch declared.

"Only thing 'round here gettin' whipped's the general's horse," Jonah replied, steppin' in front of me and puttin' his nose in the captain's face. "Leave us be, Cap'n. We know what to do!"

Fitch started grumblin' 'bout Texican discipline, but I drew out my bowie knife, and the rest of the company seemed eager to join the fray. Captain Fitch shouted orders, but even the boys he'd brought out from Kentucky refused to heed him.

"Guess we gone and unelected you, Cap'n," Jonah declared.

But later, when we called 'round for somebody else to take over, nobody stepped forward. So we were Fitch's company still, though there weren't many of us left.

Mosely Baker's and Wily Martin's commands joined up with us that day, and their men talked of shootin' 'cross the Brazos and droppin' a few Mexicans.

"Sesma's sure to be on our heels," one of Martin's boys said. "And Urrea's got cavalry down south toward Velasco."

It wasn't warmin' news. Pretty soon we could find ourselves cut off and forced to fight—on Santa Anna's terms.

"One thing, though," Jonah told me as we stood together in company formation. "Won't be anybody surrenderin'. Not after Goliad."

I nodded grimly. We were all of us out of sorts, ill-tempered, and downright angry. I guess that's why Mosely Baker set after the general.

"You said you didn't attack the Mexicans on the Colorado because you didn't have any artillery!" Captain Baker bellowed. "Now you got two brand spanking new cannon and yet you didn't stand and fight at the Brazos. Are you going to Harrisburg or not?"

Of course that wasn't what Baker was askin'. He wanted to know if we'd fight. The rest of us did, too, and that night it was pretty much decided the army would, General Houston or not!

★104★

"There's a fork in the road yonder," Jonah told me. "Left fork takes you east, to the Sabine. Right one goes down toward Harrisburg, to Lynch's Ferry at Buffalo Bayou. There's a call goin' 'round to go right no matter what the officers do. And we'll stand and wait for Santa Anna and shoot Mexicans long as we're able."

I remembered Buck Travis's words: "Victory or death." I didn't envy him much, as dyin' wasn't apt to bring much pleasure. But we were tired of marchin', and we were mad. I figured it was time to make a stand, even if it was to die.

The general had the civilians out ahead for once, and we all watched in dismay as they turned left at the fork. You could hear the sad notes of travelin' songs and the weepin' of widows and orphans leavin' their homes forever. Wily Martin's company followed as escort, but the rest of the army went right. You could feel the shiver workin' through us, passin' into a surge of fresh spirits. Wasn't anytime 'fore we were cheerin' this officer and that. We even gave ole Fitch a holler, and he wasn't worth a snail's shell.

If we needed spurrin', a Mexican colonel named Almonte took care of it. He sent General Houston a note by way of a black man on a mule.

"Mr. Houston, I know you're up there hiding in the bushes," the message read. "As soon as I catch the other land thieves I'm coming up to smoke you out."

"Land thieves?" I cried. "Better that than a liar and murderer."

We were all a little too mad to be good soldiers, but we soon had a laugh to settle us. Seems the general borrowed some oxen from a certain Miz Mann to haul the cannon along. Now up rode Miz Mann, cussin' up a storm, with a pistol on one hip and a bowie knife on the other.

"Sir, I want my oxen!" she yelled.

"Well, Mrs. Mann, we can't spare them," Houston answered. "We can't get our cannon along without them."

"I don't care about your cannon. I want my oxen!" Without so much as a wink she bent over, took her knife, and cut loose those oxen. She whipped 'em 'long homeward, and we all swapped grins.

"General, we can't get along without those oxen," Captain Rogers, who was seein' after the guns, declared. "The cannon are bogged down."

"Well, we have to get along the best we can," the general replied.

"General, I'll go to bring the oxen back!" Captain Rogers shouted, turnin' his horse and startin' the pursuit.

"Captain, that woman'll fight!" the general warned.

"Confound her fightin'!" the captain answered. "We need those oxen!"

"Now there's a man to fight for," Jonah declared as the captain rode off.

"Maybe," I admitted. "But I'll bet you he comes back without any oxen. I seen women with that same look before. Miz Mann's sure to have her way."

The general clearly thought so, too, for he had a dozen men set to movin' the guns along. Later that night Captain Rogers came back empty-handed, and we had another laugh.

"Hey, Cap'n, where's your oxen?" someone called.

"She wouldn't let me have 'em," he explained.

"How'd your shirt get tore?" another soldier asked.

"Likely cut it off'n him to use for baby rags," somebody else suggested.

We had a high time makin' up tales 'bout Captain Rogers's battle with Miz Mann. We hadn't had much to eat again, and the night was damp and chilled. Those stories warmed us for a while.

We got to Buffalo Bayou across from Harrisburg on April 18, and General Houston sent out scouts to find the Mexicans. Ole Deaf Smith, a peculiar sort of fellow who was off ridin' ahead or behind us most days and was thought by some of us more phantom'n human, rode in to say Santa Anna was down on San Jacinto Bay—close by. Then Deaf hurried over to Harrisburg and caught a Mexican courier. The rider was a full captain, and he carried all manner of dispatches scribbled by General Filasola and intended for El Presidente himself.

The capture was a thing of importance, of course, for it helped the general considerable to know what the Mexicans were up to. We were more roused by Deaf Smith, though. He went and swapped his muddy buckskin britches and coonskin cap for that Mexican captain's big sombrero and fine woolen pants. That Mexican was a sight, with his bemedaled shirt and big shoulder boards. Deaf's cap near covered his face, though, and the muddy pants didn't fit at all.

"Now we're sure to lick Santy Anny," one old-timer judged. "Deaf Smith's gone and stole their best hat!"

General Houston, meanwhile, walked off to study the dispatches. He had some of the Spanish speakers among the army give him a hand in translatin' the words. Then Houston stomped 'round, slappin' at his thigh like a man possessed. Before we knew it, he'd called out orders to march again. This time I saw in his eyes he meant to close with Santa Anna. Whether it was Almonte's note or the captured dispatches or the temperament of the army set him in motion, he appeared a changed man. And we were an army once more.

Before leavin' Harrisburg, the officers gave a look after

the sick. We'd had a fresh outbreak of measles, and there was fear the whole army might come down with it. I was rollin' up our tent when I noticed a gaggle of red spots on Jonah's forehead.

"Oh, Lord," he gasped as he saw more spots on his arms.

"You gone and caught chicken pox," I told him.

"Can't be," he argued.

"I'm one to know. I had 'em myself, and I nursed a sister and three brothers through the same thing."

Captain Fitch said as much when he sent Jonah to the sick camp. Altogether two hundred men were left there, plus a small guard to keep watch over 'em and see to the army's baggage and what few prisoners we'd taken 'round Harrisburg.

"Looks like you'll have to fight Santa Anna on your own," Jonah told me 'fore leavin'.

I nodded sadly. His words tore through me, for I realized I truly was alone. Billy, Noah, Jonah—they were all gone now. So was Zach. And my family? Mama was in New Orleans, but as to J. C., Ruth Alice, and the boys, who knew?

The army formed up in a hollow square opposite Buffalo Bayou. General Houston and Tom Rusk together took the center. The general, taller'n usual ridin' a fine white stud, Saracen, pointed south toward Harrisburg where a pillar of smoke rose to stain the mornin' sky.

"Santa Anna's burning another Texas town," Houston told us. We saw the smoke, gritted our teeth, and prepared to hear the words that were sure to send us to battle.

"Victory is certain!" Houston shouted. "Trust in God and fear not! The victims of the Alamo and the names of those who were murdered at Goliad cry out for cool, deliberate vengeance. Remember the Alamo! Remember Goliad!"

Others took up the cry. Some cried, "Remember La Bahía," usin' the name of the Goliad fort. Some of the Spanish speakers in Captain Seguin's company called, *"Recuerden el Alamo!"* It all meant the same. And on the faces of those surroundin' me, I saw recollections of friends like Zach who were there in spirit.

I believe just then we'd've charged through the fires of perdition if the general'd led us on that big white horse.

"It's no use looking for aid," the general warned. "None is at hand. Colonel Rusk is with us. I rejoice in this."

Rusk took his cue and spoke to us, too.

"Santa Anna is just below us, within the sound of a drum," the redhead shouted. "A few more hours will decide the fate of the army."

He went on 'bout how many good Texans were absent, but we knew that. Some were sick. Others were tendin' families. A lot were skedaddlin'.

"May I not survive if we don't win this battle!" Rusk concluded. A cheer rose, and the colonel announced he was done. Again the cries, "Remember the Alamo. Remember Goliad!" erupted from the army.

We were in a fever pitch, and nothin' on God's earth could've held us back.

The scouts swam their horses across the bayou, followed by the cavalry. General Houston crossed on a sort of raft. The rest of us took an ole ferry. It was none too stable, and when it lurched to one side, I fell hard against a splintery nail and ripped open the side of my trousers.

"Looks like you're wounded, Tim," a fellow named James Duncan observed, pullin' a splinter out of my hip. "And exposed, too."

"I got a needle," an old-timer we called Uncle Jack said, and he mended my trousers 'fore we got across the bayou. "Don't feel bad, son. The general went and did the same thing, I hear. Only he didn't get such fancy stitchwork."

"Thanks, Uncle Jack," I told him.

"You done good stickin' with us when so many stayed behind," he declared. "When the shootin' starts, you stay at my elbow, hear? I fought Indians and cow thieves aplenty, and you don't do much good gettin' yourself kilt."

"Guess not," I replied.

"Lost my own nephews at Goliad," he then whispered. "Just got out here from Georgia, eager to be heroes. Didn't even get a chance to pray over their graves."

"I lost a friend at the Alamo," I explained.

"Be a day of vengeance comin', Tim boy. A day heaven's been waitin' for!"

We marched a way to Lynch's Ferry. There was a cluster of folks on the far side, and we thought them reinforcements for a time.

"Santanistas," one of Seguin's men announced as they melted away. "Come to welcome El Presidente."

I guess that made us madder'n anythin'. As General Houston fanned us out among the moss-strewn oaks on the southeast fringe of a field boundin' the bayou, I asked Uncle Jack where we were.

"It's called the field of San Jacinto," he told me. "I figure it'll be a place long remembered."

THIRTEEN

Wednesday, April 20 was a chill, grayish sort of day. We were spread out in the trees like a batch of angry hornets just waitin' for somebody to sting. Colonel Sherman was given charge of the second regiment, and they were over on the left, eager to fight. Colonel James Neill and the Twin Sisters were in the middle, with the guns maybe ten paces in front of the trees lest some bit of smokin' waddin' set the forest ablaze. Captain Fitch's company, all fifteen of us, served with Ned Burleson's regiment, the First Texas. To our side was a small band of what was called regulars, mostly American soldiers who'd taken a kind of furlough from their posts in Louisiana to give Texas a hand in gettin' born. They carried the army's solitary banner. Some of us joked the flag was a reminder of what we held most dear. There was a near naked Miz Liberty on it, wavin' a sword. It had "Liberty or Death" scrawled on it, but I think the soldiers meant the lady more'n the motto.

Off to our far right the cavalry stood at the ready. It was near impossible to see most of us, and I expect the general planned it that way. If the Mexicans saw how few of us were left, they'd sweep us right into the bayou and be done with it. This way they might settle down to a rifle duel, and our marksmanship would serve us well in that sort of fight.

"It's a good position," Uncle Jack told me. "Water on the flanks, and in back, too. They got to come at us head-on."

I supposed it was an advantage since he thought it so, but I had to steady myself every few minutes against the notion of thousands of Mexicans chargin' us with gleamin' bayonets.

It was Colonel Sherman who first rode off to have a look after Santa Anna. He returned at a gallop, and James Duncan remarked, "Guess the colonel found what he was after."

We laughed a bit, but it wasn't easy laughter. Sure enough the Mexicans came up on the horizon, cavalry in the vanguard, followed by the long columns of infantry. The horsemen then peeled off to one side, and skirmishers broke out from the main force and started forward. Buglers took up a sour, hauntin' refrain, and Uncle Jack spit.

"What is it?" I asked.

" 'Degüello,' " he explained. "Beheadin' song. Played it at the Alamo, I heard. Means no quarter's to be given."

"And none asked," James Duncan added angrily.

The Mexican army was a model of good order. A band of cavalry rode forward to cover the approach of this big cannon. Uncle Jack vowed it was a twelve-pounder and was certain to outrange the Sisters. It did, too, for its first shot landed back in the bayou. The Twin Sisters answered with a shower of broken horseshoes—the closest thing we had to cannon balls.

The Mexicans moved their cannon closer and fired again. This time the shot bounced and hit Colonel Neill in the backside, knockin' him down. Our gunners yelled angrily, and for a time the battle was little more'n a gunner's duel. All this time a tall Mexican on a big horse rode back and forth among the skirmishers, shoutin' orders and wavin' his hands about. He was decked out in all sorts of gold braid, with a fancy French hat atop his head.

"It's him," Uncle Jack said, pointin' to the fellow. "El Presidente himself!"

The news brought us to life. More'n one Texican tried a rifle shot at Santa Anna, but he took care to keep movin'. And though a shot or two dropped a skirmisher, the Butcher of Bexar rode on unharmed.

"He's showin' his men he's not afraid," James noted.

"Let him just come a little closer," Uncle Jack begged. "I'll make certain he's never feared again."

Colonel Sherman, who had no patience at all, rounded up sixty or so horsemen and made a rush for the Mexican cannon. Santa Anna'd been ready for that 'cause he dispatched the whole of the Mexican cavalry after Sherman. There was a brief clash of arms before the weight of the Mexican lancers began to press our men back. Tom Rusk was out there, and he would've been killed for sure if that same Lamar who wanted to raid General Gaona from the *Yellowstone* hadn't gone to the rescue. Lamar seemed everywhere. He saved Rusk, then shot down a lancer about to impale young Walt Lane. As Lamar pulled Lane up behind him and raced off, even the Mexican cavalry applauded. Lamar wasn't one to miss a chance to show off, and he stopped a moment and bowed to the enemy.

Santa Anna responded to the foolishness by orderin' the "Degüello" blown again.

We'd surely have had the battle then and there, but Santa Anna pulled back his men. The Mexicans busied themselves throwin' up a barricade of saddles and such and made camp back of it.

"Why should he fight today when he's got reinforcements comin'?" Uncle Jack said. "Be better to hit 'em early tomorrow, when the sun's in their eyes. That's how I'd do it."

I wondered what had become of the riflemen's duel. But I was tired and hungry, and news we'd captured a flatboat full of supplies bound for the Mexicans swept other thoughts away. For the first time in ages we had plenty of coffee and flour. I mixed up dough and baked bread on a stick while Uncle Jack cut strips of beef and dangled 'em over the coals. I filled our coffeepot, too, and we sat 'round the fire, warmin' ourselves against the night while smellin' the scent of bubblin' coffee and bakin' bread.

It was good we got some rest and ate well, for that night a blue norther hit Texas. The wind whined across Buffalo Bayou and cut through our bones. We huddled in the trees, wishin' we had our tents or even a few blankets. Finally, exhausted, I fell asleep and dreamed of a warm bed back in New Orleans.

Dick, a big black freedman, beat reveille 'round nine that next mornin'. We could hear celebratin' in the Mexican camp, and word passed among us that General Cos had arrived with another thousand men.

"Don't you worry over them," Captain Fitch announced. "They'll be too tired from the march to fight."

I looked at him cross-ways. We'd done enough marchin' to know you got used to it. Another thousand rifles—or bayonets—didn't improve our odds.

The weather began to clear as we ate our breakfast. Meanwhile the Mexican cavalry formed up little more'n a quarter mile away.

"Looks to be a fine day to fight a battle, boys!" General Houston shouted as he made his way among the men. But though he sent Deaf Smith and the other scouts off to chop down a bridge and cut off Mexican reinforcement—or their retreat—he didn't seem in a hurry to get the fightin' started. We'd lost the advantage of the sun by now, and some were grumblin' we'd skedaddle all over again. As it turned out, Houston was just waitin' to hear the bridge was down and for Smith to count the enemy.

"Two thousand, somebody says," James whispered. "And Filasola and Urrea are closin' in."

I shuddered at the thought of five or six thousand Mexican regulars lined up opposite our cold, half-starved regiments. But 'round three o'clock the general ordered the men formed. Without much more'n a wave of his hand, General Sam Houston climbed atop Saracen and led the way out across the open ground that lay between us and the Mexican army.

Our seven hundred ragged soldiers formed a line two men, then one man deep. We spread out in a crescent nine hundred yards across and stared at the Mexican barricade. We didn't spy a single Mexican. Not a one!

Suddenly Dick, the drummer, and a German fifer took up playin' a tune, and I winced. Seemed best, after all, to leave the Mexicans sleepin', or doin' whatever distracted 'em from our approach. On top of all that, they were playin' a bawdy tune, "Will you come to the bow'r?" It was popular enough at Mr. Lott's tavern, but it seemed we should march to battle singin' a hymn or some such. So it was we walked on, raisin' our voices in a devil of a tune and spurred on by a flag bearin' the likeness of some naked female!

Over in Company D, Mosely Baker was shoutin', "Neither ask nor give quarter!" One of his soldiers stuck a red kerchief on his rifle barrel and waved it like a flag. We had no "Degüello."

"Trail arms," the general barked. Then, leadin' us on his big white stud, he yelled, "Forward!"

The artillery was over to the right now, supported by both the cavalry and the regulars. They hauled the Twin Sisters by rawhide straps toward the silent Mexican camp. General Houston rode ahead of the army thirty yards or so, callin', "Hold your fire until we crest the hill."

We were maybe three hundred yards away when the enemy opened fire. Their muskets weren't much use at that range, and their cannon overshot us.

"Hold your fire!" the officers shouted. "Don't waste powder."

"Wasn't goin' to waste it," Uncle Jack muttered when Captain Fitch ordered him to shoulder his rifle. "I aimed to kill me a Santanista."

We came closer still. A man to my right fell, shot through the knee.

"Halt!" Houston yelled. "Halt. Now is the critical time. Fire away! Aren't you going to fire?"

Actually there wasn't much to fire at save the general himself. The Twin Sisters opened up, though, rippin' holes in the barricade and fillin' the air with cries from Mexican dead and wounded.

"Now!" Captain Fitch yelled. At last we could detect the heads and shoulders of a small band of Mexicans crouchin' on the low breastwork, and we took aim. Uncle Jack fired first, and a Mexican fell backward. I aimed at a stumpy fellow to the right and set the trigger. As I pulled it, the rifle discharged, and my eyes stung from the powder smoke. I looked back, and the whole wall had been swept with rifle fire. We gave a yell and raced ahead.

We fell on the barricade like madmen, surged up and over and into the Mexican camp. Those of the enemy who managed to reach the barricade gave us a fair fight. The general's horse was shot, and later, at the breastwork, a second horse was holed and Houston himself took a copper ball in his right leg. It didn't stop him, though, and we followed his example into the camp, usin' our rifles as clubs, flashin' knives, kickin' and clawin' and screamin', "Remember the Alamo! Remember Goliad!"

"Recuerden el Alamo!" Seguin's company shouted. And the Mexicans broke and ran.

After the barricade, you couldn't really call it a fight. No, it was murder, pure and simple. Mexican soldiers stumbled out of their tents and were shot down in their nightshirts. Some threw up their arms and cried, *"Me no Alamo. No Bahía!"* It didn't matter. There was too much fire in our blood. I don't know if I killed the stumpy Mexican on the barricade, but I did shoot a skinny fellow who was fumblin' with his musket over beside a supply wagon. My bullet went through his side and up into his chest. He turned and stared a moment before dyin'. I froze, but Uncle Jack pulled me along.

"They're gettin' away," he yelled. "Come on. Let's go."

I would've let 'em if it'd been up to me, but I knew he was right. We had a chance to defeat Santa Anna here and now, and those that got away would come back like Cos had returned after Bexar. Uncle Jack and I joined a line of riflemen that was closin' in on half a Mexican battalion that some colonel managed to form. We let loose a volley into 'em, and the officer fell. Two young lieutenants, one of them little older'n me, urged the men to stand, but a second volley shattered their line, and we charged into what was left, clubbin' and slashin' till there wasn't a Mexican left standin'. The boy lieutenant was cut up worse'n a butchered hog, and I stared at his empty eyes and thought of Zach. Then I walked over behind a supply wagon and was sick.

When my eyes regained their focus, I saw I wasn't alone. Three Mexican soldiers cowered beneath the wagon, and a young bugler stared up at me in panic. He made the sign of the cross and bowed his head, expectin' the worst. The soldiers tossed their muskets aside and raised their hands.

"Come on," I said, motionin' with my rifle for 'em to follow. They got to their feet and marched solemnly back toward the barricade. I didn't know what else to do with 'em. The flag was flyin' there, and I hoped somebody would be in charge. If I went out onto the plain where the fightin' went on, somebody was sure to kill the four of 'em. Mosely Baker wasn't the only one yellin', "No quarter."

We were a comical sight, I suppose. That long rifle was at least as big as I was, and my clothes, long coated with mud, now showed traces of powder smoke and blood. I'd torn off the right leg of my trousers crossin' the barricade, and my bare knee showed up pale white against the rest of me. As for my captives, only the bugler had all his clothes. Two of the others marched in their drawers, and one was wrapped in a sheet. You'd've thought I'd caught 'em bathin' in a creek!

When I neared the flag, I saw one large tent had been converted into a hospital. We'd lost a few men, and others were shot. Mostly the wounded were Mexicans, though. Nearby, some Texas soldiers kept watch over a sulkin' band of prisoners.

"Here are four more," I told a bearded sergeant.

"Got a little one, eh?" the sergeant asked, jabbin' the

bugler in his ribs. "Ain't started shavin' yet!" He then peered at me, and laughed. "Guess we got some youngsters with us, too, eh?"

The three riflemen quickly took their places among the other prisoners. The bugler paused, then dropped to his knees and kissed my hand.

"*Gracias, tejano,*" he said, sobbin'. He then tore open his collar and removed a small silver crucifix. He handed it to me, but I shook my head.

"Keep it," I argued. "You're sure to need it more'n me."

As I turned to leave, he sat with his older comrades and wept.

"Should've taken the cross," the sergeant told me. "Somebody sure will. He'd taken it better givin' it away, don't you think?"

I scowled. In the distance rifle fire continued to tear at the afternoon sky, and I hurried to rejoin the fightin'.

Mostly the battle was over. Bands of soldiers ferreted out Mexicans here and there. They were hidin' everywhere, especially the officers. Even with their medals flung aside and their shoulder boards ripped off, they were recognized by their shaven faces and manicured hands. The private soldiers fared the worst, though. Perhaps they brought to the Texicans' minds the butchery at Goliad, how the last survivors of the Alamo had been bayoneted. You could see in their faces they expected no mercy, and Texican riflemen stood alongside the bayou shootin' 'em down for another hour. Others, fleein' into deep water, drowned.

"You, what company are you assigned?" a captain called.

"Cap'n Fitch's company," I answered. "I don't recall the letter."

"Well, you're with Company F for now," the captain announced. "Help us collect all these muskets and side arms. With this damp weather, they're certain to rust if we don't. And I dislike the notion of some Mexicans comin' back after dusk and stealin' their guns back so as to shoot us in the dark."

"Yes, sir," I said, givin' him a brisk salute. I was glad of the chance to put my hands to better purpose, and I noticed many of the younger soldiers were doin' the same. There was another company siftin' through baggage, carryin' linens to the hospital tent for the doctors to use. Once the shootin' finally stopped, others helped us gather the arms. Most of the men took to gatherin' mementos, though, or exchangin' their worn-out moccasins for Mexican boots.

By nightfall a degree of order was fallin' over the battlefield. The prisoners, some seven hundred of them, were penned up. The Twin Sisters, primed and ready to fire, stared down at them. In addition, a guard was posted, but it was clear most of the captives had been purged of the will to fight. They bowed politely and thanked us for their rations, and when some of the Texicans brought 'em blankets, they smiled and offered up prayers.

I paid a visit to the young bugler. He seemed glad to see me and managed a smile. His face was bruised, and his shirt was torn open so that his chest was bare. I noticed the cross gone and recalled the sergeant's words. Someone had taken the boy's boots, too, along with his trousers. He was wearin' some ill-fittin' buckskins, but he didn't complain. Instead he softly blew a melody on his horn and rattled off a fair parade of Spanish. I didn't digest all of it, but I understood him ask about a brother, Felipe Ramirez, who was not among the prisoners. He was a lieutenant, it seemed, and was perhaps wounded. I paid a visit to the hospital, but they had no such person there.

"I know of Ramirez," a Mexican officer called. I turned and explained the purpose of my inquiry. "Ah, I have only sadness for you to share," the officer said in perfect English. "Felipe fell fighting with General Castrillón. He died bravely."

I thanked him and returned to the prisoner pen. My Spanish was poor, and I managed only to blurt out Felipe's name and add, *"Muerto."*

The boy dropped his chin to his chest and cried. Between sobs he explained their other brother and their two uncles had fallen at Bexar, stormin' the Alamo. I thought of Zach again, but I had no hardness left in me for the bugler. I knew what it was like to be alone.

I left him to his sadness and located my company. Uncle Jack raced over, lifted me off my feet, and hugged me like a long-lost brother.

"Lord, Tim, we thought you dead!" he shouted. "I looked 'round and you were gone."

"There's coffee on the fire," James told me. "Lots of beef to fry up, too. We got a skillet from the Mexican camp and a good tent you're welcome to share. Looks like we best find you some britches, too. Even Uncle Jack won't sew those back together."

Uncle Jack led me over to the fire, and a couple of the others managed to fix me some supper. I had little appetite, but I did chew a biscuit and wash some beef down with coffee.

"Try these here," James said a bit later, bringin' me some trousers and a Mexican lancer's dress shirt. The shirt fit fair enough, but the trousers were big by a hand and a half. He set off again and returned shortly with a pair that fit near perfect. "Got you this, too," he added, handin' me a beautiful pistol and a knapsack full of odds and ends. "Figure to stay 'round for the end?"

"The end?" I asked.

"Got to find Santa Anna," Uncle Jack explained. "He got away, him and Cos both. We got Deaf Smith out lookin', and some of the boys set off with dogs. The butchers'll turn up."

"Guess so," I muttered.

"Had your fill of soldierin', eh?" James asked.

"Of killin', anyway."

"It's all war is," Uncle Jack declared. "Funny part's how once the shootin' stops, you look 'round and see these Mexican fellows ain't so very different. They'd make good enough neighbors if it wasn't for scoundrels like Santa Anna sendin' 'em down here to murder us and burn our towns."

"No, they're not so different," I agreed, recallin' the face of the bugler.

"If you was to go back to Washington anytime soon, you could do us a service," James finally said. "When we went through the tents we come across a sword with Cap'n Stewart's name on it. I know Billy'd be happy to have it, and we got together some silver coins, too. Make it easier for him and the family. You bein' a good friend of his, I thought you might pass 'em on."

"I'd like to, only the war's not over."

"Well, it will be," Uncle Jack declared. "I heard the Mexican officers talkin'. They got no heart to keep fightin', not after Santa Anna bleedin' his army at Bexar and now gettin' half of it torn to pieces at San Jacinto. What's left won't be in too high a fever to fight on. And we're sure to nab him ourselves tomorrow."

"I figure Cap'n Fitch'll give you furlough, Tim," James

explained. "We can get you a horse and have you out of here tomorrow. What do you think?"

"I think I'd like that," I confessed. "If the cap'n ..."

"He'll do what we tell him," Uncle Jack insisted. "Or be unelected again."

I grinned at them and warmed my hands over the flame. There was a scent of powder and death on the wind. I'd be glad to quit the place.

It was only hours later, as I lay atop a captured Mexican blanket, that I recalled the date. It was April 21.

"Know what, Uncle Jack?" I whispered.

"What, Tim?"

"I'm fifteen today. It's my birthday."

"Texas's, too, I'm thinkin'," he told me. "Now get to sleep with you."

FOURTEEN

I AWOKE to find the sun hangin' high in the midmornin' sky. I hadn't slept so late in years, and never durin' my weeks in the Texas army. I poked my head outside the tent and found soldiers sittin' 'round takin' long sips from wine bottles or whiskey jugs captured from the Mexicans. Others played cards, mended torn clothes, or swapped tales. Some were already gettin' their belongin's together, for there was talk of issuin' many their discharge.

"What's happened?" I asked Uncle Jack when I located him off by the bayou washin' bloodstains out of captured clothes.

"Don't you know?" he asked. "They drug in El Presidente. Dressed like a field hand, all save his diamond-studded shirt. His own soldiers gave him away. Seems for sure Santa Anna'll sign a treaty. If nothin' else, he'll do it to save his hide. Plenty of the men would opt for stretchin' his neck or fryin' his gizzard, either one."

Mostly we Texicans patched ourselves up and scoured the woods for more prisoners. Cos was still loose, and there were sure to be others. Every so often a band of horsemen rode in draggin' a man or two. There were still those in the army who preferred huntin' their unfortunate enemy like wild game than roundin' 'em up as captives.

There was a good deal of work to be done in camp, too. A fair amount of loot remained, and now the officers took charge to see it was sorted and listed. Tents were struck, and horses driven off to fresh grass. The takin's were considerable. Some six hundred muskets, three hundred sabers, two hundred pistols, seven hundred mules and horses, some twelve thousand dollars cash, and eighty wagonloads of shot and powder were accounted for. And that was after the army had taken its share.

As for the dead, General Houston wanted the Mexican prisoners to bury 'em, but Santa Anna refused.

"Told Cap'n Seguin to let 'em rot," Uncle Jack explained.

I thought all the worse of El Presidente for that. Those men were ill-led, but they'd fought bravely. Lorenzo de Zavala came to take the corpse of General Castrillón, an old friend. Others known in Texas were recognized and dutifully buried. I tried to locate Felipe Ramirez and get him covered up, but most of the bodies were stripped to their drawers or were downright naked, and what with 'em bein' shot or cut up, there was no recognizin' one from the other.

The stench was considerable, too, and our company moved its camp back to the live oaks where the breeze off the bayou sweetened the air. The sky was alive with buzzards, and it sickened me to think of what those men'd look like come summer.

"Be a fierce sight," Uncle Jack remarked. "Sure to make an enemy think twice 'fore he sets his sights on invadin' Texas."

I suppose that was true, and clearly our small army would be hard-pressed to bury so many. Some suggested buildin' a bonfire, but there was scant wood handy, and it seemed a poor reward to those live oaks that had concealed us to burn 'em after the battle.

I stayed in the army till Saturday, April 23. By then Cos had been located, dapper and gregarious in his moment of defeat, and Santa Anna had ordered Generals Gaona, Filasola, and Urrea to withdraw their troops—first to Bexar and then across the Rio Grande, as Texicans took to callin' the Bravo. That was to be the new Republic's border with Mexico, by all I heard.

With peace seemingly at hand, many of the men asked to go see after their families. Others, especially young ones like me, were discharged altogether. I managed to get myself a Mexican horse and five silver dollars, together with a discharge that promised me six hundred forty acres of land in the north or west.

I rode home past the blackened remains of San Felipe, past wagons full of others returnin' now Santa Anna was beaten at San Jacinto.

"You were there, were you?" people cried. "You, a boy, drove the Mexican army into the bayou!"

Some doubted my tale, but it wasn't hard to prove. I was even then wearin' my lancer's shirt and Mexican trousers. With a pistol and bowie knife tucked in my belt and a rifle slung across the rump of my horse, who was goin' to argue anyway?

I was a week gettin' up the Brazos to the ferry. When I appeared on the eastern bank, together with two wagons bound for Gonzales, I grinned from ear to ear. The ferry was there like always, and ole Jupe was wearily startin' across.

He didn't see me at first, and I kept myself behind a woman and her two daughters.

"Any charge for a hero of San Jacinto?" I asked.

"What?" he asked, raisin' an eyebrow. "Who say that?"

"Me," I announced, steppin' out so he could see.

"Tim Piper, you's a sight!" he bellowed. The others started to grumble, but Jupiter ignored 'em. Instead he gave my horse a stroke and lifted me high onto his broad shoulder. "Lord, you been good to Jupe this day. Praise and glory, Tim, you come back."

"We're eager to cross," a passenger complained.

"Can't you see the boy's come home to his family?" Jupe cried. "Been off fightin' with General Houston, he has. Got himself a fine new outfit of clothes."

"And stories to share," I said. "But I think first we better get these folks across."

"Well, come ahead on," he barked. I led my horse onto the ferry and tied him securely. Then I helped guide the first wagon aboard. The second we'd bring next trip.

"Give me a piece of that line and we'll quicken the trip," I suggested.

"Was wonderin' if soldierin' went and made you lazy," he said as he moved over and let me help pull the ferry to the west bank.

Afterward, I excused myself, tied the horse to a nearby post oak, and raced on up the hill to see the others. J. C. was mendin' a loose plank on the porch, and he near hammered his finger when he caught sight of me.

"Timmy!" he called, rushin' over and wrappin' me up in his powerful arms. "Lord, you've grown, I believe."

"Been to war," I told him. "And lived to get back home."

We stood face to face for a moment, and I noticed I didn't have to gaze up quite so much as when I'd first arrived. Ruth Alice ran out to join us, and she hugged me tightly and cried on my shoulder.

"You're home for good, aren't you?" she whispered.

"Till I'm a bit bigger," I answered. "I've got six hundred forty acres of land comin', you know. Might start my own farm 'fore long."

"Not too soon, though," she urged.

"I've got a trip to make to the Stewart place, too," I told her. "And I need to see Noah Hayes. Jonah's come home already, I heard."

She nodded, and I sighed with relief to know my friends, too, had survived military life.

"Tim's home!" Leander shouted then, and he and Titus ran over and began tuggin' at the pistol in my belt.

"He's got a Mexican soldier's shirt on, too," Titus observed.

"You'll tell us all 'bout it, won't you, Timmy?" Leander pleaded. "Won't you?"

"Maybe," I answered, gazin' past the trees in the direction of Zach's farm. "When the recollectin's not so sharp. For now I'm home. I figure that means I can forget it for a time."

"Sure it does," J. C. said. "It means there's work to do, and that there'll be hot water for you to wash with come dusk. And later, a warm bed and good company."

I smiled.

"You'll write your mama, too," Ruth Alice insisted. "Tell your family you're all right."

"I am, too," I told her. "Now I'm home."

Acknowledgments

All historical fiction relies first and foremost on the events that it portrays, the chroniclers who recorded them, and the historians who preserve them for us. *Piper's Ferry* is especially indebted to the diaries of William Physick Zuber and John Holland Jenkins—both of whom were teenage soldiers in the army of the infant Republic of Texas—and to the more elaborate writings of Colonel William Fairfax Gray, who witnessed the Washington Convention in his travels and recorded so well life in Austin's colony. For the Mexican viewpoint, I looked to José Enrique de La Peña's *With Santa Anna in Texas*, developed from the diaries Peña kept while a staff officer serving with Santa Anna in Texas.

Others have written in this century of the dramatic events in Texas, notably Frank X. Tolbert in *The Day at San Jacinto* and T. R. Fehrenbach in *Lone Star*. But I also relied on countless shorter articles published over the years, especially between the Centennial celebration of 1936 and the Texas Sesquicentennial of 1986.

While researching *Piper's Ferry* I had the good fortune to meet Ellen N. Murry, curator of education at the Star of the Republic Museum at Washington-on-the-Brazos. For her help in steering me in the right direction and allowing me access to the museum library and artifacts, I am eternally grateful. From "The Star of the Republic Museum Notes," which Ellen edited, I accumulated information on the day-to-day habits of settlers on the Texas frontier.

Texas is blessed with many fine testaments to its troubled beginnings, and visitors can still visit a replica of Independence Hall at Washington-on-the-Brazos, tour Sam Houston's homes in Huntsville, and explore the reconstructed walls of Presidio La Bahía at Goliad and the Alamo at San Antonio (Bexar). A solitary column near Coleto Creek and a more elaborate graveside marker attest to Colonel Fannin's failure. For Buck Travis and the Alamo heroes, there is no headstone. At these sites, and at Gonzales and San Jacinto, both state and local groups have preserved the evidence of the Texas Revolution. To them I am grateful for the labor of love they have performed. To the Daughters of the Republic of Texas, who deem it their special duty to keep strong the images of the past, I pay special tribute.

Finally and especially I am grateful to the librarians in my old hometown of Garland and my new home, Plano, for their help in tracking down hard-to-find resource books. Without them many pieces of the puzzle would have remained missing.

G. Clifton Wisler
Plano, Texas

About the Author

Author G. Clifton Wisler grew up on tales of Davy Crockett and the heroes of the Alamo. He says: "The idea for *Piper's Ferry* came on one of my many visits to old Washington-on-the-Brazos and the Star of the Republic Museum. I'd been accumulating a file drawer full of research material, together with a few hundred photographs. But it wasn't until stumbling across some letters written by a young Texan to his mother back in New Orleans that Tim Piper came to life."

An award-winning author, Mr. Wisler has written more than thirty-five novels, many of them for young people. A near-lifelong resident of Texas, he now lives in Plano.